Books by
MEG CABOT

ALL-AMERICAN GIRL

READY OR NOT: AN ALL-AMERICAN GIRL NOVEL

TEEN IDOL

AVALON HIGH

AVALON HIGH: CORONATION #1:
THE MERLIN PROPHECY (MANGA)

HOW TO BE POPULAR

PANTS ON FIRE

JINX

NICOLA AND THE VISCOUNT

VICTORIA AND THE ROGUE

THE BOY NEXT DOOR

BOY MEETS GIRL

EVERY BOY'S GOT ONE

SIZE 12 IS NOT FAT

SIZE 14 IS NOT FAT EITHER

QUEEN OF BABBLE

QUEEN OF BABBLE IN THE BIG CITY

BIG BONED

The Mediator Books:

THE MEDIATOR 1: SHADOWLAND

THE MEDIATOR 2: NINTH KEY

THE MEDIATOR 3: REUNION

THE MEDIATOR 4: DARKEST HOUR

THE MEDIATOR 5: HAUNTED

THE MEDIATOR 6: TWILIGHT

MEG CABOT

HARPER TEEN
An Imprint of HarperCollins*Publishers*

HarperTeen is an imprint of HarperCollins Publishers

Jinx
Copyright © 2007 by Meg Cabot, LLC.
All rights reserved. Printed in the United States of America.
No part of this book may be used or reproduced in any manner what-
soever without written permission except in the case of brief quota-
tions embodied in critical articles and reviews. For information
address HarperCollins Children's Books, a division of HarperCollins
Publishers, 1350 Avenue of the Americas, New York, NY 10019.
www.harperteen.com

Library of Congress Cataloging-in-Publication Data
Cabot, Meg.
    Jinx / Meg Cabot—1st ed.
        p.   cm.
    Summary: Sixteen-year-old Jean "Jinx" Honeychurch, the descen-
dant of a witch, must leave Iowa to live with relatives in Manhattan
after the first spell she casts goes awry, but she will have to improve
her skills to stop her cousin from practicing black magic that endan-
gers them and the boy they both like.
    ISBN 978-0-06-083764-8 (trade bdg.)
    ISBN 978-0-06-083765-5 (lib. bdg.)
    [1. Witchcraft—Fiction.   2. Cousins—Fiction.   3. High schools—
Fiction.   4. Schools—Fiction.   5. Wealth—Fiction.   6. New York
(N.Y.)—Fiction.]   I. Title.
PZ7.C11165Jin 2007   2006100448
[Fic]—dc22

Typography by Sasha Illingworth
1 2 3 4 5 6 7 8 9 10
❖
First Edition

For Benjamin

Acknowledgments

Many thanks to Beth Ader, Jennifer Brown,
Michele Jaffe, Laura Langlie, Amanda Maciel,
Abigail McAden, and especially Benjamin Egnatz

CHAPTER ONE

The thing is, my luck's always been rotten. Just look at my name: Jean. Not Jean Marie, or Jeanine, or Jeanette, or even Jeanne. Just Jean. Did you know in France, they name *boys* Jean? It's French for John.

And okay, I don't live in France. But still. I'm basically a girl named John. If I lived in France, anyway.

This is the kind of luck I have. The kind of luck I've had since before Mom even filled out my birth certificate.

So it wasn't any big surprise to me when the cab driver didn't help me with my suitcase. I'd already had to endure arriving at the airport to find no one there to greet me, and then got no answer to my many phone calls, asking where my aunt and uncle were. Did they not want me after all? Had they changed their minds? Had they heard about my bad luck—all the way from Iowa—and decided they didn't want any of it to rub off on them?

But even if that were true—and as I'd told myself a million times since arriving at baggage claim, where they were supposed to have met me, and seeing no one but skycaps and limo drivers with little signs with everyone's names on them but mine—there was nothing I could do about it. I certainly couldn't go home. It was New York City—and Aunt Evelyn and Uncle Ted's house—or bust.

So when the cab driver, instead of getting out and helping me with my bags, just pushed a little button so that the trunk popped open a few inches, it wasn't the worst thing that had ever happened to me. It wasn't even the worst thing that had happened to me that *day*.

I pulled out my bags, each of which had to weigh fifty thousand pounds, at least—except my violin case, of course—and then closed the trunk again, all while standing in the middle of East Sixty-ninth Street, with a line of cars behind me, honking impatiently because they couldn't pass, due to the fact that there was a Stanley Steemer van double-parked across the street from my aunt and uncle's building.

Why me? Really. I'd like to know.

The cab pulled away so fast, I practically had to leap between two parked cars to keep from getting run over. The honking stopped as the line of cars that had been waiting behind the cab started moving again, their drivers all throwing me dirty looks as they went by.

It was all the dirty looks that did it—made me realize I was really in New York City. At last.

And yeah, I'd seen the skyline from the cab as it crossed the Triboro Bridge . . . the island of Manhattan, in all its gritty glory, with the Empire State Building sticking up from the middle of it like a big glittery middle finger.

But the dirty looks were what really cinched it. No one back in Hancock would ever have been that mean to someone who was clearly from out of town.

Not that all that many people visit Hancock. But whatever.

Then there was the street I was standing on. It was one of those streets that look exactly like the ones they always show on TV when they're trying to let you know something is set in New York. Like on *Law and Order*. You know, the narrow three- or four-story brownstones with the brightly painted front doors and the stone stoops. . . .

According to my mom, most brownstones in New York City were originally single-family homes when they were built way back in the 1800s. But now they've been divided up into apartments, so that there's one—or sometimes even two or more families—per floor.

Not Mom's sister Evelyn's brownstone, though. Aunt Evelyn and Uncle Ted Gardiner own all four floors of their brownstone. That's practically one floor per person, since Aunt Evelyn and Uncle Ted only have three kids, my cousins Tory, Teddy, and Alice.

Back home, we just have two floors, but there are seven people living on them. And only one bathroom.

Not that I'm complaining. Still, ever since my sister Courtney discovered blow-outs, it's been pretty grim at home.

But as tall as my aunt and uncle's house was, it was really narrow—just three windows across. Still, it was a very pretty townhouse, painted gray, with lighter gray trim. The door was a bright, cheerful yellow. There were yellow flower boxes along the base of each window, flower boxes from which bright red—and obviously newly planted, since it was only the middle of April, and not quite warm enough for them—geraniums spilled.

It was nice to know that, even in a sophisticated city like New York, people still realized how homey and welcoming a box of geraniums could be. The sight of those geraniums cheered me up a little.

Like maybe Aunt Evelyn and Uncle Ted just forgot I was arriving today, and hadn't deliberately failed to meet me at the airport because they'd changed their minds about letting me come to stay.

Like everything was going to be all right, after all.

Yeah. With my luck, probably not.

I started up the steps to the front door of 326 East Sixty-ninth Street, then realized I couldn't make it with both bags and my violin. Leaving one bag on the sidewalk, I dragged the other up the steps with me, my violin tucked under one arm. I deposited the first suitcase and my violin case at the top of the steps, then hurried back down for the second suitcase, which I'd left on the sidewalk.

Only I guess I took the steps a little too fast, since I

nearly tripped and fell flat on my face on the sidewalk. I managed to catch myself at the last moment by grabbing some of the wrought-iron fencing the Gardiners had put up around their trash cans. As I hung there, a little stunned from my near catastrophe, a stylishly dressed old lady walking what appeared to be a rat on a leash (only it must have been a dog, since it was wearing a tartan coat) passed by and shook her head at me. Like I'd taken a nosedive down the Gardiners' front steps on purpose to startle her, or something.

Back in Hancock, if a person had seen someone else almost fall down the stairs—even someone like me, who nearly falls down the stairs every single day—they would have said something like, "Are you all right?"

In Manhattan, however, things were clearly different.

It wasn't until the old lady and her pet rat passed all the way by that I heard a click. Straightening—and finding that my hands were covered in rust from where I'd gripped the fence—I saw that the door to 326 East Sixty-ninth Street had opened, and that a young, pretty, blond girl was peering down at me from the top of the stoop.

"Hello?" she said curiously.

I forgot about the old lady and her rat and my near-pavement-dive. I smiled and hurried back up the steps. Even though I couldn't quite believe how much she'd changed, I was so glad to see her—

—and was so worried she wasn't going to feel the same way about seeing me.

"Hi," I said. "Hi, Tory."

The young woman, very petite and very blond, blinked at me without recognition.

"No," she said. "No, I am not Tory. I am Petra." For the first time, I noticed that the girl had an accent . . . a European one. "I am the Gardiners' au pair."

"Oh," I said uncertainly. No one had said anything to me about an au pair. Fortunately, I knew what one was, because of an episode of *Law and Order* I saw once, where the au pair was suspected of killing the kid she was supposed to be watching.

I stretched my rust-stained right hand out toward Petra. "Hi," I said. "I'm Jean Honeychurch. Evelyn Gardiner is my aunt. . . ."

"Jean?" Petra had reached out and automatically taken my hand. Now her grasp on it tightened. "Oh, you mean Jinx?"

I winced, and not just at the girl's hard grip—she was really strong for someone so little.

No, I winced because my reputation had so clearly preceded me, if the au pair knew me as Jinx instead of Jean.

"Right," I said. Because what else could I do? So much for getting a fresh new start in a place where no one knew me by my less-than-flattering nickname. "My family calls me Jinx."

And would continue to do so forever, if I couldn't turn my luck around.

CHAPTER TWO

"But you are not supposed to arrive until tomorrow!" Petra cried.

The tight ball of worry in my stomach loosened. Just a little.

I should have known. I should have known Aunt Evelyn wouldn't have completely forgotten about me.

"No," I said. "Today. I'm supposed to arrive today."

"Oh, no," Petra said, still shaking my hand up and down. My fingers were losing all circulation. Also, the places I'd skinned grabbing the wrought-iron fence weren't feeling too good, either. "I'm sure your aunt and uncle said tomorrow. Oh! They will be so upset! They were going to meet you at the airport. Alice even made a sign. . . . Did you come all this way by yourself? In a taxi? I am so sorry for you! Oh, my goodness, come in, come in!"

With a heartiness that belied her delicate frame—but

matched her handshake—Petra insisted on grabbing both of my bags, leaving my violin to me, and carrying them inside herself. Their extreme heaviness didn't seem to bother her at all, and it only took me a couple of minutes to find out why, Petra being almost as big a talker as my best friend, Stacy, back home: Petra had moved from her native Germany to the United States because she's studying to be a physical therapist.

In fact, she told me she goes to physical therapy school every morning in Westchester, which is a suburb just outside of New York City, where, when she's not in class, she has to lift heavy people and help them into spas, then teach them to use their arms and stuff again, after an accident or stroke.

Which explained why she was so strong. Because of the lifting of heavy patients, and all.

Petra was living with the Gardiners, paying for her room and board by caring for my younger cousins. Then, while the kids were in school every day, she went to Westchester to learn more physical therapy stuff. In another year, she'll have her license and can get a job in a rehabilitation center.

"The Gardiners have been *so* kind to me," Petra said, carrying my suitcases to a third-floor guest room as if they didn't weigh more than a couple of CDs.

It didn't even seem like it was necessary for Petra to take a breath between sentences. Amazingly, English was not even her first language.

Which meant she could probably speak faster in her native tongue.

"They even pay me three hundred dollars a week," Petra went on. "Imagine, living in Manhattan rent-free, with all of your food paid for as well, and someone giving you three hundred dollars a week! My friends back home in Bonn say it is too good to be true. Mr. and Mrs. Gardiner are like a mother and father to me now. And I love Teddy and Alice like they are my own children. Well, I am only twenty, and Teddy is ten, so I guess he could not be my son. But my own little brother, maybe. Here, now. Here is your room."

My room? I peered around the doorframe. Judging by the glimpses I'd had of the rest of the house on our way up the stairs, I knew I was going to be living in the lap of luxury for the next few months. . . .

But the room in which Petra set my bags down took my breath away. It was totally beautiful . . . white-walled with cream-and-gilt furniture, and pink silk drapes. There was a marble fireplace on one side—"It does not work, this one," Petra informed me sadly, like I had been counting on a working fireplace in my new bedroom, or something—and a private bathroom on the other. Sunlight filtered through the windows, making a dappled pattern on the light pink carpeting.

Of course, I knew right away something was wrong. This was the nicest bedroom I'd ever seen. It was a hundred times nicer than my bedroom back home. And I'd had to share that bedroom with Courtney and Sarabeth, my two younger sisters. This would, in fact, be my first time sleeping in a room of my own.

EVER.

And never in my life had I so much as entertained the idea of having my own bathroom.

This was just not possible.

But I could tell from the casual way Petra was going around, flicking imaginary dust off things, that it *was* possible. Not just possible, but . . . the way things were.

"Wow," was all I could say. It was the first word I'd been able to get in since Petra had begun speaking, down at the front door.

"Yes," Petra said. She thought I meant the room. But really, I'd meant . . . well, *everything*. "It is very nice, yes? I have my own apartment in this house, with a private entrance—downstairs, you know? The ground floor. You probably did not see it. The door is underneath the stoop to the townhouse. There is also a back door to the garden. It is a little private apartment. I have my own kitchen, too. The children come down at night sometimes, and I help them with their homework, and sometimes we watch the TV together, all snug. It is very nice."

"You're not kidding," I breathed. Mom had told me that Aunt Evelyn and her family were doing well—her husband, my uncle Ted, had recently gotten a promotion to president of whatever company it was he worked for, while Evelyn, an interior decorator, had added a couple of supermodels to her client list.

Still, nothing could have prepared me for . . . this.

And it was mine. All mine.

Well, for the time being, anyway. Until I messed it up, somehow.

And, me being me, I knew that wouldn't take long. But I could still enjoy it while it lasted.

"Mr. and Mrs. Gardiner will be so sorry they were not home to greet you," Petra was saying as she went to the side of the king-sized bed and began fastidiously fluffing the half-dozen pillows beneath the tufted headboard. "And they'll be even sadder that they got the days mixed up. They are both still at work. Teddy and Alice will be home from school soon, though. They are both very excited their cousin Jinx is coming to stay. Alice has made you a sign to welcome you. She was going to hold it at the airport when they greeted you, but now . . . well, perhaps you could hang it on the wall here in your room? You must pretend to be pleased by it, even if you are not, because she worked very hard on it. Mrs. Gardiner did not put anything on your walls, you see, because she wanted to wait to see what you are like. She says it has been five years since they last saw you!"

Petra looked at me in wonder. Apparently, families in Germany lived a lot closer and visited one another a lot more often than families in the U.S. . . . or *my* family, anyway.

I nodded. "Yes, that sounds about right. Aunt Evelyn and Uncle Ted last came to visit when I was eleven. . . ." My voice trailed off. That's because I'd just noticed that in the massive bathroom, the fixtures were all brass and shaped like swan necks, with the water coming out of the bird's carved beak. Even the towel bar had swan wings on the ends. My mouth was starting to feel a little dry at the sight of all this luxury. I mean, what had I ever done to deserve all this?

Nothing. Especially lately.

Which was actually why I was in New York.

"What about Tory?" I asked, in an effort to change the subject. Better not to think about why it is I'm here in New York and not back in Hancock. Especially since every time I did, that pesky knot in my stomach clenched. "When does she get home from school?"

"Oh," Petra said.

This "Oh," however, was different from all the others Petra had let out. I noticed right away. Also, whereas before Petra had been speaking with undisguised enthusiasm, now she looked down and said uneasily, with a shrug, "Oh, Tory is home from school already. She is in the back, in the garden, with her friends."

Petra pointed toward one of the two windows across from the bed. I went over to it, gingerly pushing aside the filmy white curtain liner—it was as fine as a spiderweb—and looked down . . .

. . . into an enchanted fairy garden.

Or at least, that's what it looked like to me. And okay, I'm used to our backyard in Hancock, which is completely filled with my younger brothers' and sisters' bikes and plastic toys, a swing set, a dog run, Mom's motley vegetable patch, and large piles of dirt, dumped there by Dad, who is forever working on a new addition to the house, which has never quite gotten done.

This backyard, however, looked like something from a TV show. And *not Law and Order*, either, but something along the lines of *MTV Cribs*. Walled on three sides by moss-covered brick, roses were growing—and blooming—everywhere. There were even rose vines wrapped around the sides of a small, glassed-in gazebo over in one corner of the garden. There was a wrought-iron table surrounded by chairs, and a cushioned chaise longue beneath the sweeping branches of a newly budding weeping willow.

But best of all was a low fountain, which, even with the windows closed three stories up, I could hear burbling. A stone mermaid sat in the center of the five-foot-wide pool, with water shooting up out of the mouth of a fish she was holding in her arms. I couldn't be sure, being so high up, but I thought I saw a few flashes of orange within the pool. Goldfish!

"Koi," Petra corrected me, when I said it out loud. Her voice was getting back to normal, now that we weren't discussing Tory, I couldn't help noticing. "They are Japanese. And do you see Mouche, the Gardiners' little cat? She sits there all day long, watching them. She has not caught one yet, but she will, one day."

I saw the sudden flare of a match being struck beneath the glass roof of the gazebo. You couldn't really see in, because the glass was frosted. Tory and her friends must have been inside, but I couldn't see them, just their shadowy movements, and the flame.

It appeared that Tory and her friends were smoking.

That's all right, though. I know plenty of people our age back in Iowa who smoke.

Well, okay. One.

Still, everyone had told me things were really different in New York. Not just things, but people, too. People my age, especially. Like, people my age in New York are supposed to be way more sophisticated and older for their age than people back home.

And that's okay. I can handle that.

Although my stomach, judging by the way it had suddenly turned back into a knot, seemed to disagree.

"I guess I should go down and say hi to Tory," I said . . . because I felt like I had to.

"Yes," Petra said. "I suppose you should." She sounded like there was something she wanted to say, but for the first time since I'd met her, she went mute instead.

Great. So what was up between her and Tory?

And what did you want to bet that, with my luck, I was going to walk into the middle of it?

"Well," I said, more bravely than I felt, letting the curtain liner drop back into place. "Would you mind showing me the way?"

"Of course."

Petra, it appeared, wasn't the type of girl to stay quiet for long. As we went down the stairs to the second floor, she asked about the violin. "You are playing it long?"

"Since I was six," I said.

"Six! Then you must be very good! We will have a concert some night, yes? The children will love this."

I kind of doubted this, unless my cousins were really different from the kids back home. Nobody I know in Hancock likes listening to me play. Except maybe when I do "The Devil Went Down to Georgia." But even then, they kind of lose interest, unless I sing the words. And it's hard to sing and play at the same time. Even Patti Scialfa, Bruce Springsteen's wife, who can play the violin and sing, never really does both at the same time.

Then Petra asked if I was hungry, and told me about the cooking class Mrs. Gardiner had paid for her to go to, so that she could learn to make American food for the children.

"I was to make filet mignon for your arrival tomorrow, but now you are here, and I think for dinner tonight, we are having Chinese food from Szechuan Palace! I hope you are not minding. Mr. and Mrs. Gardiner have a benefit they have to attend. The Gardiners are very kind, giving people, and are always going to benefits to raise money for worthy causes . . . there are many of these in New York City. And Chinese food here is very good, it is authentic—Mrs. Gardiner even says so, and she and Mr. Gardiner have been to China for their anniversary last year—Oh, here is the door to the garden. I guess I will be seeing you, then."

"Thanks, Petra," I said, giving her a grateful smile.

Then I slipped out the glass door that led to the patio overlooking the garden, and went down the steps to the garden itself (clinging carefully to the wrought-iron rail to avoid a second near-disaster with a set of stairs).

Here the sound of the fountain was much louder, and I could smell the heavy scent of roses in the air. It was weird to be in the middle of New York City and smelling roses.

Although intermingled with the rose smell was the scent of burning tobacco.

I called out, "Hello?" as I approached the gazebo, to let them know I was coming. No one responded right away, but I was pretty sure I heard someone say the F word. I figured Tory and her friends were scrambling to stamp out their cigarettes.

I hurried to enter the gazebo, so I could say, "Uh, don't worry. It's only me."

But of course I found myself speaking to six total and complete strangers. My cousin Tory wasn't anywhere to be seen.

Which is, you know. Just my luck.

CHAPTER THREE

Then one of the strangers, a girl whose jet-black hair matched the color of her minidress and high-heeled boots, came swaggering out of the gazebo and stood with one hand on a narrow, jutting hip while she eyed me suspiciously through heavily made-up eyes.

"Who the hell are you?" she demanded.

Aware that the people inside the gazebo were staring at me with equal hostility, I heard myself stammer, "Um, I'm Jean Honeychurch, Tory Gardiner's cousin. . . ."

The black-haired girl said the F word again, this time in quite a different tone. Then she lifted the hand she'd been keeping behind her back, and took a long swig from the glass she held. "Don't worry," she said, over her shoulder to the people in the gazebo. "It's just my freakin' cousin from Iowa."

I blinked, once. Twice. And then a third time. *"Tory?"* I asked incredulously.

"Torrance," my cousin corrected me. Setting the glass down on a low stone bench, she pulled a cigarette out from behind her ear and wedged it between her scarlet lips. "What are you doing here? You weren't supposed to come until tomorrow."

"I . . . I guess I'm early," I said. "Sorry."

Don't even ask me why I was apologizing for something that wasn't even my fault—the Gardiners were the ones who'd got the day of my arrival wrong, not me.

But there was something about Tory—this new Tory, anyway—that made the knot in my stomach twist harder than ever. *This* was Tory? *This* was my cousin Tory, with whom, when the Gardiners had last come to visit us in Iowa, I'd waded down in Pike Creek, and climbed trees over by the elementary school?

It couldn't be. *That* Tory had been pudgy and blond, with an impish smile and an equally mischievous sense of humor.

This Tory looked as if it had been a long time—a *really* long time—since she'd last smiled.

Not that she wasn't pretty. She was, in a supersophisticated, urban-chic sort of way. She'd lost her baby fat, and now her figure was reed-slim. The blond hair was gone, too, replaced with a severely cut, ink-black pageboy.

She looked like a model—but not one of those happy, sunny ones, like Cindy Crawford. She looked like one of the pouty, unhappy ones . . . like Kate Moss, after she'd gotten busted for doing all that cocaine.

Tory, I wanted to say. *What* happened *to you?*

Tory must have been thinking something along the same lines—only about *me* having changed since she last saw me—since she suddenly chuckled (managing to make it one of the most humorless chuckles I'd ever heard) and said, "God, Jinx. You haven't changed a bit. You still look farm-fresh and country-sweet."

Oh. So maybe she *wasn't* thinking something along the same lines.

I looked down at myself. I had dressed with extra-special care that morning, knowing that when I stepped off the plane, it would be in the most sophisticated city in the world.

But evidently my jeans, pink cotton sweater, and the same-color pink suede loafers were not citified enough to disguise the fact that I am, for the most part, exactly what Tory had accused me of being: farm-fresh and country-sweet.

Although we actually live on a cul-de-sac, not a farm.

"God," said a voice from within the gazebo. "What I wouldn't give for that *hair*." And then, wriggling like a snake, a girl every bit as model-slim as Tory—Tyra to Tory's Kate Moss—slipped from the gazebo, and joined Tory in her inspection of me.

"Is this *natural*?" the girl asked, standing on her toes in order to take hold of one of the curly red tendrils that spring from my head with an abandon I've basically given up trying to contain. She seemed to be wearing some kind of school uniform made up of a white blouse, blue blazer, and pleated gray skirt.

But on her, even a school uniform looked like high fashion. That's how pretty she was.

"Oh, her hair's natural," Tory said—not like she thought it was a good thing, either. "Our grandmother has it, too."

"God," the girl said. "That is so wild. I know girls who pay *hundreds* to get spiral curls like that. And the color! It's so . . . *vivid.*"

"Hey," said a masculine voice from the gazebo. "Are you girls just gonna squeal over Red over there, or are we gonna get down to business?"

The girl who had liked my hair rolled her eyes, and even Tory—or Torrance, as she apparently now preferred to be called—cracked something that resembled a smile.

"God, Shawn," she said. "Relax." To me, she said, "You want a beer?"

I tried not to let my shock show. A beer? Tory was offering me a beer? Tory, who five years ago wouldn't even eat Pop Rocks, because she was convinced they would make her stomach explode?

"Um," I said. "No, thank you." Not because I don't drink—I had champagne at Stacy's mom's wedding to her new stepdad, Ray—but because I don't like beer.

"We've got a pitcher of Long Island iced tea, too," Tory's friend said in a friendly way.

"Oh," I said, feeling relieved. "Okay. I'll have some of that."

Tory's friend made a face. "Yeah," she said. "I don't

20

like beer, either. I'm Chanelle, by the way."

"Chanel?" I repeated. I wasn't sure I'd heard her right.

"Right," she said. "Only with an extra L and E at the end. Chanel's my mom's favorite store."

"Good thing it wasn't Gucci," the boy Tory had called Shawn said.

"Ignore him," Chanelle said to me, rolling her expressive dark eyes again, as I followed her into the gazebo. "That's Shawn," she said, pointing to a blond guy who was seated at a glass-topped table inside. He had on gray trousers, a white dress shirt with the sleeves rolled up, and a red-and-blue-striped tie, which had been carelessly knotted, and just as carelessly loosened again.

"And that's my boyfriend, Robert, over there," Chanelle went on. Another boy, this one dark-haired, but wearing exactly the same clothes as Shawn, nodded at me over the cigarette he was rolling.

Which was when I realized it wasn't a cigarette at all.

"And that's Gretchen," Chanelle said, pointing at another model-pretty girl—this one blond, with a pierced eyebrow—wearing the same uniform as Chanelle. "And that's Lindsey." Lindsey, also in school uniform, was a smaller version of Gretchen, minus the piercing. Instead, she was wearing a velvet choker and bright red lipstick.

Both girls barely acknowledged my existence. They looked way more interested in the drinks they held than in me.

"Okay," Shawn said, rubbing his hands together. "We

done with the chitchat now? Can we get back down to business?"

In the farthest corner of the gazebo, over where the glass wall met up with the brick one, someone cleared his throat.

"Oh," Chanelle said. "I almost forgot. That's Zach."

The guy in the corner tipped a can of Coke in my direction as a sort of salute. "Hello, Cousin Jean from Iowa," he said pleasantly. He, unlike the other two boys, wasn't wearing a tie or dress slacks, but jeans and a T-shirt. He was also, I thought, a good year or two older than everyone else in the gazebo, who looked more or less my age.

He was also hot. Way hot. In your average wide-shouldered, dark-haired, green-eyed, Greek-god kind of way.

"Weren't you leaving, man?" Shawn asked Zach . . . and not in a very friendly voice.

"I was going to," Zach said, moving over to make room for me on his bench—the only seat left. "But maybe I'll stick around a bit longer."

"Suit yourself," Shawn said. But he didn't sound too happy about it.

"Good," Tory said, pouring a glass of iced tea from a pitcher that sat on the gazebo floor. She passed the glass to me. I'd taken the seat next to Zach. "I hate how you never stick around to party, Zach."

"Maybe I'm just not that into copping a buzz before dark," Zach said.

"I wish I could be buzzed twenty-four seven," Robert

said wistfully, as he licked the ends of his rolling paper.

"You are," Chanelle assured him. And not like she was pleased about it, either.

"Okay, where were we?" Tory wanted to know. "Oh, yeah. I need at least enough to get me through midterms. How about you, Chanelle?"

"Well," Chanelle said. I noticed that the sweater she had tied around her waist was the same color blue as the stripes in the boys' ties. So were Gretchen's and Lindsey's.

So they all went to the same school—the Chapman School, which I was transferring into . . . a bit late in the year, admittedly. But there'd been extenuating circumstances.

I swallowed. Better not to think of the extenuating circumstances right now.

"None for me, thanks," Chanelle said.

"God, Chanelle," Tory said, her lip curled. "Midterms. Not to mention, spring formal. Do you want to be a heifer at it? Hello?"

"God, Torrance. Blackheads. Not to mention, zits. Do you want my dermatologist to kill me? Hello?" Chanelle shot back, not unpleasantly, and in a dead-on imitation of Tory that made Lindsey snort until iced tea came out of her nose.

"Loser," Tory said, when she saw this. Lindsey wiped her nose on her sweater sleeve, and said, "Put me down for twenty."

"Twenty," Shawn said, punching numbers into the

Treo he'd pulled from a backpack sitting on the floor. "You, Tor?"

"Same, I guess," Tory said.

She lit her own cigarette, studiously ignoring me, even though I was looking right at her. I couldn't believe what I was seeing. I mean, it was bad enough Tory was a brunette now, and thin as a movie star. But she was buying drugs, too? Although I had to admit, Shawn didn't look anything like the drug dealers they show so regularly on *Law and Order*. He wasn't superskinny or wearing dirty clothes. He looked . . . *nice*.

And Tory didn't look like a junkie. I mean, she's totally gorgeous.

Still, her life, at least so far as I could tell, seemed perfect. What did she need drugs for?

These were the thoughts that were banging around in my head as I sat there. I guess you could say I was suffering from some major culture shock.

Also, the knot in my stomach was bigger and tighter than ever.

"And I need some Valium," Tory added. "I've been very tense lately."

"I thought that's what your little trips with Shawn down to the boiler room during free study were for," Gretchen said, speaking up for the first time. Her voice was surprisingly gravelly.

So was what she was saying. Surprising, I mean. Tory and Shawn were going out?

But Tory just shot her friend a sarcastic look. And her middle finger.

"I can get you ten," Shawn said, grinning. "Any more'n that is just askin' for trouble. I know it's a lost cause, but how about you, Rosen? Need anything?"

Beside me, Zach said, "No, thanks. I'm good."

Tory looked shocked. "Zach," she said. "Are you sure? Because Shawn can get the real thing, you know. None of that generic crap. His dad's a doctor."

"Jesus, Tor, the man's straight, all right? Leave him alone," Shawn said. His gaze settled on me. "How 'bout you, Red?"

Tory, who'd looked annoyed a moment earlier, laughed so hard that some of her drink went up her nose, and she started choking. This made Lindsey say, "Loser," exactly the way Tory had when it had happened to her.

I said, trying not to show how completely freaked out I was, "No, thank you. I'm—I'm trying to quit."

"Hey," Zach dead-panned. "Good for you, Cousin Jean. The first step is admitting you've got a problem."

"Thanks," I said, and tried to hide my mortification that the hottest guy in the room was talking to me by taking a sip of my iced tea . . .

. . . which I promptly spat out.

Unfortunately, all over Zach.

"Hey," Robert said, clutching his joint defensively. "Say it, don't spray it, Red!"

"Oh my God," I cried. I could feel my cheeks going up

in flames. "I'm so sorry. I didn't realize . . . I didn't expect there to be—"

"—alcohol in it?" Tory had recovered herself, and now she threw a handful of napkins at Zach. "Why do you think it's called a *Long Island* iced tea, moron?"

"I've never had one before," I said. "I've never even been to Long Island. Oh my God, Zach, I'm so sorry."

But Zach didn't look mad. In fact, he had a bemused smile on his face. "'I've never even been to Long Island,'" he echoed, as if he were trying to memorize the phrase.

"I'm so sorry," I said again. I really couldn't believe it. I mean, I *could*, because it was so typical of me, of course. But I also couldn't because—well, because I had just spat Long Island iced tea all over the cutest boy I had ever seen. I mean, I'd been in New York barely an hour, and already, I'd made a complete ass of myself. Tory and her friends had to think I was the worst backwater hick they'd ever met. It wasn't like none of the kids from school back home ever drank, or got high, or bought drugs.

They just didn't tend to do it . . . well, around me.

"I really am sorry," I said.

Zach grinned at me. I felt a pluck on my heartstrings. Steady there, Jean.

"No problem, Cousin Jean from Iowa. You want a Coke, or something?" The grin grew broader. "And I do mean the carbonated kind."

"Sure," I said, completely dazzled by the smile. "That'd be great."

Zach rose, but sat down again when Tory barked,

"*I'll* get it for her," and abruptly marched out of the gazebo.

"Jesus," Gretchen said. "What's with *her*?"

Robert rolled his eyes in Zach's direction. "Take a wild guess."

"What?" Chanelle demanded, defensive on Tory's account.

"Jesus, are you all blind? The Torster's onto Rosen," Robert said, between puffs.

Zach frowned. "What do you mean, Tory's onto me?"

"The au pair, man." Robert shook his head. "Why else would a big important junior like yourself hang around with us lowly sophomores? You're obviously not here to buy, so . . ."

Zach, rather than denying this, as I half expected him to, just looked thoughtful.

"Hey," Chanelle said indignantly. "That's not true. Torrance is into Shawn. She isn't crushing on Zach."

"If Tor's so into Shawn," Robert wanted to know, "why's she trying so hard to keep Rosen away from the au pair? Huh?"

"Shut up, Robert," Chanelle said, giving him a kick under the glass-topped table. "You don't know what you're talking about."

"Hey, don't shoot the messenger," Robert said. "The Torster's got it so bad for Mr. Four-Point-Oh over here, she can already taste—if you know what I mean."

"Gross!" Chanelle cried, and even Zach frowned disapprovingly and said, "Not in front of Cousin Jean, please. She's new here."

Robert looked over at me. "Oh," he said. "Sorry."

And I felt like dying even more than ever. *Cousin Jean?* It was almost as bad as *Jinx*.

Almost.

"Hey, it's all good. Torrance and I," Shawn said mildly, looking up from his Treo, "have an agreement."

It was at that exact moment that Tory came back with a can of soda. "Here, Jinx," she said, shoving the soda at me. "What kind of agreement do we have, Shawn?"

"You know," Shawn said. His fingers were flying over the keypad of his Treo, his gaze glued to the screen. "Open relationship, and all that crap."

"Oh," Tory said, sinking back into her seat. "Right. Friends with benefits. Why are we talking about this?"

"No reason," Chanelle said quickly, glaring at Robert, who just smirked.

I sat there, trying not to look shocked. Friends with benefits? I tried to picture what my best friend Stacy would do if her boyfriend, Mike, suggested to her that they be friends with benefits, instead of an exclusive couple.

Then I shuddered. Because the resulting bloodshed, I knew, would not be pretty.

"By the way," Tory said to me, breaking in on my thoughts. "You're welcome."

"Oh," I said, looking down at the soda can that sat, forgotten, in my hand, and feeling myself turning red again. "Thanks."

"You'll find many more just like it in the fridge," Tory said meaningfully. "Did Petra show you the kitchen?"

"Not yet—"

"Well, make sure you get a tour. This is the last time I fetch and carry for you."

"God, Tor," Chanelle said. "Be a bitch, why don't you?" Then, as if embarrassed by Tory's rudeness, Chanelle turned to me, and asked, "So how long are you visiting New York, Jean?"

The knot in my stomach lurched. I looked back down at my can of Coke.

"I'm transferring to Chapman for the rest of the school year," I said. "And then spending the summer here, too."

I didn't miss the glances Gretchen and Lindsey exchanged. Not that I blamed them. Who transfers into a new school with only one month left in the semester?

A freak like me, that's who.

"Right," Tory said airily. "I forgot to tell you guys. Jinx here'll be finishing out the semester with us."

"Why?" Chanelle wanted to know.

On the one hand, I was relieved Tory apparently hadn't told them about me. Now I could tell them whatever I wanted about why I was here.

On the other hand, I was also kind of hurt. Which was ridiculous, of course.

But you would think she might have mentioned to her friends that her cousin was coming to live with her. Unless, of course, it simply wasn't that important to her.

"Oh," I said, swallowing. "I just kind of needed a change."

Tory rolled her eyes. "God, Jinx," she said. "Could you maybe think of something lamer to say when people ask you that? They're going to, you know. A lot."

Wow. So much for my being able to tell them whatever I wanted about why I was here.

I felt myself blush. Again.

"Well," I said. The knot in my stomach was turning into less of a knot, and more of a fist. "It's kind of . . . personal."

"For God's sake," Tory said, snatching the joint from Shawn and taking a long pull on it. "Just tell them. Jinx is being stalked, okay?"

CHAPTER FOUR

Great. Just great.

I will admit it, I should have known better. I should have had an answer to Chanelle's very natural question all prepped and ready.

Only I didn't. Of *course*.

So I guess I deserved what Tory had just given me.

But at the same time, it was a shock to hear her say it like that, so matter-of-factly.

Especially since that was only the half of it. The other half, of course, was known only to me.

Thank God. Because I wouldn't have put it past Tory to blurt that part out, too, if she'd only known about it.

Especially since she seemed to be loving the reaction she was getting—my mortified silence, and Gretchen's and Lindsey's gasps.

Shawn said, "No shit?" and even Zach, I noticed, turned his green-eyed gaze on me in a manner that made me feel even more uncomfortable than I did already.

Chanelle's eyes were wide. "Really?" she said. "Stalked? That must be scary."

"You're so lucky!" Lindsey squealed, giggling. "I've never been stalked. What's it like?"

"God." Tory stamped the joint out into an ashtray on the glass table. "There's nothing exciting about it, Lindsey, you idiot. I hear the guy's a complete psycho. He'll probably come here and murder us all in our beds. I can't believe my parents even agreed to this."

"Hey," Robert said, outraged. "That joint was still good!"

I couldn't believe it, either. Not about the joint. But that Tory could have just . . . ANNOUNCED it that way, so casually. Especially considering the fact that I'd had to leave home, and all my friends, and the school in which, I'll admit, I'd been pretty popular. I mean, I'm a *nice* girl. People like nice girls. These kinds of things don't happen to nice girls. Nice girls don't get stalked . . .

. . . unless, of course, they happen to bring it on themselves.

But Tory didn't know that part of it.

So for her to just blurt out the part she did know like that . . .

And in front of Zach, too, who was making my heartstrings twang practically every time I looked at him.

I wanted to die again. Or throw up. It was hard to decide which.

"He's not a stalker," I said, choosing my words with care. And also realizing, from the startled looks people threw me, that maybe I'd said it a little too loudly. I lowered my voice. "He's not psycho, either. He's just a guy I went out with, who got a little too serious, too fast."

There, how did that sound? Would they believe it? Please let them believe it. . . .

"He probably wanted to hold hands," Tory said, straight-faced, and Shawn snorted with laughter.

Okay. Well, that was mean.

But they believed it. *Tory* believed it, anyway.

And that was all that mattered.

When I shot her a dirty look for the holding hands remark—because I felt like that's what a girl like me would do—Tory said, "Well, come on, Jinx. Your mom IS a minister."

Chanelle flung me a startled look. "No way! You're a PREACHER's daughter?"

Of course she said it like it was a bad thing. People always do.

"I'm also a computer consultant's daughter," I said. "My dad works with computers."

But no one was listening. No one ever does.

"God," Lindsey said. "That is so romantic. You had to flee the state in order to escape an obsessive lover. I wish *I* had an obsessive lover."

"I wouldn't mind a sober one," Chanelle said dryly. "Instead, I just have Robert."

Robert looked up from the joint he was trying to salvage. "What?" he said, when he saw everyone was staring at him.

"See what I mean?" Chanelle asked, with such a twinkle in her dark eyes that I couldn't resist laughing—

—until Shawn burst out with, "What is this? Freaking *Oprah*? Enough with the new girl's love life. I need payment, ladies." He held out his Treo, so they could read the total on it. "And, no, I do not take personal checks."

Tory scowled, but reached for her purse. A Prada, the thousand-dollar one from the new spring line my sister Courtney had told our parents was the only thing she wanted for her birthday. Mom and Dad had laughed like it was the funniest thing they'd ever heard.

Tory and Gretchen and Lindsey each counted out a short stack of twenty-dollar bills. Then, shoving the cash toward her boyfriend, Tory asked, "When can we expect delivery?"

"Tomorrow," Shawn said, gathering up the money and shaking it into a neat little pile before putting it into his wallet. "Monday at the latest."

"Tomorrow," Tory said, her eyes narrowing.

"All right, all right." Shawn shook his head. "Tomorrow."

"Torrance?" Petra's voice called from the patio. "Torrance, your mother's on the phone!"

"Crap," Tory said. "I'll be right back."

This, I knew, was my cue to make a graceful exit. Well, not graceful, knowing me. But an exit, anyway.

"I should go, too," I said, getting up. "I have a lot of unpacking to do. It was really nice to meet all of you."

I wasn't sure if this was the right thing to say to a bunch of jaded New York City teens. But Chanelle said cheerfully, "Nice meeting you, too. See you in school!"

So I guess it was okay.

"And I," Zach said, also rising, "hear my calculus homework calling. See you guys later."

"Torrance!" Petra called again.

Tory swore and left the gazebo. Zach followed her, and I followed Zach. While the back view of Zach was every bit as impressive as the front view of him had been, I couldn't enjoy it. All I wanted to do was go up to my pretty pink room and shut the door and stay there for a while, alone, with my nonworking marble fireplace, and figure out what had just happened—not to mention, what I was going to do.

Because this was not working out quite the way I'd imagined it would. Not at all. Not that I'd thought Tory and I would spend our time together wading in a creek and climbing trees. I just hadn't exactly expected . . .

Well, *this*.

On the patio, Petra handed the phone to Tory, then smiled at me and Zach.

"Hello," she said. "I see you two have met. Not going over the wall today, Zach?"

Zach held up his hands, which were, I noticed for the

first time, covered in faint pink scrapes—not unlike the ones I'd received from the wrought-iron fence I'd grabbed to keep myself from falling down earlier that day.

"Not with those roses growing so out of control back there," he said. "Those things are going to kill me one day."

"You should come in through the door like a normal person, anyway," Petra said, with a grin. "You are too old now to be climbing over walls." To me, she said, "Jean, if ever you want to see a museum, or go to the opera, or to the theater, Zach is the one to ask. He knows everything there is to know about this city—"

"Hey, come on now," Zach said, looking slightly embarrassed. Was Robert right? *Did* Zach have a crush on Petra?

But if he was in love with Petra, you couldn't tell by looking at him as he interacted with her. He seemed to treat her with as much friendly casualness as he did . . .

. . . well, me.

"It's true," Petra said, beaming at Zach. "When I first come here, and I knew no one except Mr. and Mrs. Gardiner and the children, Zachary took me *everywhere*. The Guggenheim, the Frick, the Met. Jazz clubs. Even to the *zoo*."

Zach looked even more embarrassed. "I like seals," he said to me, as if to excuse the apparent oddness of his taking the au pair to the zoo.

Hmmm. Maybe he *did* have a little crush on her.

"And then," Petra went on, as we followed her through the French doors, into the den, "when my boyfriend, Willem, came to visit, Zachary, he gave us tickets to . . . what is it called?"

"Cirque du Soleil," Zach said, now looking *completely* embarrassed. He shrugged good-naturedly, however. "My dad's always getting tickets for stuff, because of his job."

I smiled at him. I couldn't help it. I mean, besides the hotness, there was just something about him that was so . . . well, likeable. *I like seals*. I would totally have understood it if what Robert had said was true, about Tory having a little crush on Zach. I had one on him myself, and I'd only just met him.

"Jesus, Mom!" Tory's voice, from across the patio, was strident. "Are you *kidding* me? I've got stuff to do, you know."

Petra started to close the French doors. "Jean," she said quickly, "I have to go and pick up the children at school. Would you like to go with me? The children would like it so much if you did."

But Petra wasn't fast enough with the French doors, nor did her gentle voice drown out Tory's next words: "Because I've got better things to do than sit around and babysit my country-bumpkin cousin, that's why!"

The French doors clicked shut, and Petra leaned quickly against them, a panicked expression on her face. "Oh, dear," she said. "I'm sure she did not . . . I'm sure . . . Sometimes Torrance says things she does not mean, Jean."

I smiled. What else could I do?

And the truth was, my feelings weren't even hurt. At least, not that much. I was embarrassed, certainly. Especially since I'd seen Zach sort of wince, and mouth the word *Ouch* at the term *country bumpkin*.

But I was coming to grips with the fact that this Tory was not the sweet, fun Tory I remembered from five years earlier. This Tory, cold and sophisticated, was a stranger.

And really, I couldn't have cared less what some stranger had to say about me.

Honestly.

Well, okay, maybe not completely honestly.

"It's all right," I said casually. At least, I hoped it sounded casual. "She probably *does* have better things to do than babysit me. The thing that sucks is that people evidently think I *need* babysitting." I added, in case they hadn't gotten the message, "I don't."

Zach raised his dark eyebrows, but didn't say anything. I hoped he wasn't remembering the Long Island iced tea, but he probably was. Petra went on making up excuses for Tory ("She is nervous about midterms." "She has not been sleeping.") all the way to the front door. I wondered why. After all, this new Tory hadn't struck me as a person who would have wanted—much less needed—someone making excuses for her.

But maybe there were things I didn't know about "Torrance" that needed to be taken into consideration. Maybe, in spite of their beautiful garden and gold-plated bath fixtures, all was not well within the Gardiner household. At least where Tory was concerned.

"Well," Zach said, when we reached the sidewalk (I was pleased I managed successfully to maneuver the front steps without falling this time). "It was nice meeting you, Cousin Jean from Iowa. I live right next door, so I'm pretty sure we'll be seeing each other again."

Well. Now at least I understood the thing about him coming over the wall—his backyard was separated from the Gardiners' by that stone wall near the gazebo—and also how it was that he, like Tory, had had a chance to change out of his school uniform before any of the others.

"Oh, yes, you will see each other often," Petra said, her mood seemingly brighter now that we were out of the house—and away from Tory. "Jean will be going to the Chapman School for the rest of the semester."

"So I heard," Zach said, with a wink at me. "I'll see you there, then. So long, Cousin Jean from Iowa."

The wink caused another heartstring to twang. I knew I better look out.

Fortunately, he turned to go. He lived, I saw, in the townhouse to the left of the Gardiners, also four stories high, this one painted dark blue, with white trim. No flower boxes, but a brightly painted front door, this one as red as the Gardiners' geraniums.

Red as blood.

Now, why did I think that?

"Come on, Jean," Petra said, tilting her head in the

opposite direction of the one in which Zach was headed. "Teddy and Alice's school is this way."

"Just a second," I said.

Because of course I couldn't go then, while the going was still good. Oh, no. Not Jinx Honeychurch.

No, I had to stand there, rooted to the spot like the hick Tory evidently thought I was, watching Zach saunter past a car that had just pulled into one of those much-sought-after New York City parking spaces. Someone on the passenger side was opening his door to get out—

—just as a man on a ten-speed bicycle, wearing a messenger bag, came tearing down the street.

That's when a couple of things seemed to happen all at once.

First, the bike messenger veered to avoid hitting the car's open door, and would have sailed up onto the sidewalk and hit Zach . . .

. . . if I hadn't, at that exact second, thrown myself in its path to push Zach, who hadn't noticed the car, the bike, or the blood-red of the geraniums, out of the way.

Which was how I ended up getting hit by a bike messenger on my very first day in New York.

Which, if you think about it, is just my luck.

CHAPTER FIVE

"You can't even see it," Aunt Evelyn said. "Well, you can, but with a little makeup, no one will notice, I swear. And by Monday, when you start school, it's sure to be gone."

I studied my reflection in a hand mirror. The bruise above my right eyebrow was only a few hours old, and it was already purpling. From experience, I knew that by Monday, the bruise would no longer be purple, but a lovely shade of greenish yellow.

"Sure," I said, to make Aunt Evelyn feel better. "Sure it will."

"Really," Aunt Evelyn said. "I mean, if I didn't know it was there, I wouldn't notice it at all. Would you, Tory?"

Tory, seated in one of the matching pink armchairs over by the nonworking marble fireplace, said, "I can't see it."

I aimed a weak smile at her. So, it wasn't my imagination after all. Tory really *had* started being nicer to me—amazingly nicer—since my head had hit the side-walk. It had been Tory, I'd learned upon regaining con-sciousness, who'd dialed 911, after having seen the whole thing unfold from the living room window. It was Tory who'd ridden in the ambulance with me, while I was knocked out cold, since Petra still had to go pick up the younger kids. It was Tory who'd been holding my hand when I woke up, woozy and sore, in the emergency room.

And it was Tory, joined by her parents, to whom I was released later that evening, once the hospital tests revealed that I had not, in fact, suffered a concussion, and would not have to be admitted for overnight obser-vation (the bike messenger, it turned out, had escaped without a scrape—his bike hadn't even gotten that messed up).

I had no idea what had occurred to make my cousin so suddenly solicitous of my well-being. She certainly hadn't seemed to care about me before the accident. Why, just because I'd been stupid enough to get myself knocked unconscious, Tory should decide she cared about me, I couldn't imagine. If anything, I had only proved Tory's point: I really *am* a country bumpkin.

Of course, it might have had something to do with the fact that Zach had come along. To the hospital, I mean. With me. In the ambulance.

They hadn't let him into the emergency room to see me, though, on account of his not being family. And when he'd learned I'd be all right, he'd gone home.

Still. If what Robert had said out in the gazebo was true—about Tory crushing on Zach—that was a good few hours of quality time they'd had together.

But Zach wasn't around now, and Tory was *still* being nice to me. So what was up with that?

I put the mirror down and said, "Aunt Evelyn, I feel so bad. You and Uncle Ted really didn't have to stay home from your party on my account. It *is* just a little bump, after all."

"Oh, please," Aunt Evelyn said, waving her hand in a pooh-poohing gesture. "It wasn't a party, it was a boring old benefit for a boring old museum. To tell you the truth, I'm delighted you provided us with such a good excuse not to have to go."

Aunt Evelyn is my mother's younger sister, but it's hard to see any resemblance between them at all, really. The blond hair is the same, but whereas my mom wears hers in one long braid that goes down to her hip, Evelyn's is cropped into a stylish, flattering pageboy.

I've never seen my mom, who considers cosmetics frivolous—much to my sister Courtney's chagrin—wear makeup. But Aunt Evelyn had on lipstick, mascara, eye shadow—even some deliciously flowery perfume. She looked—and smelled—very glamorous and hardly old enough to have a sixteen-year-old daughter.

Which, I supposed, proved that the makeup was working.

Aunt Evelyn noticed the empty mug by the side of my bed. "You want a little more cocoa, Jean?"

"No, thank you," I said, with a laugh. "If I have any more cocoa, I'm going to float away. Really, Aunt Evelyn, you and Tory don't have to sit here with me all night. The doctor said I'm fine. It's just a bump, and believe me, I've had plenty of bumps before. I'll be all right."

"I just feel so awful," Evelyn said. "If we had only known you were coming today, and not tomorrow, like we thought—"

"You'd have what?" I asked. "Had all the bike messengers in the city locked up in advance?" Not that that would have worked. They'd still have found me. They always do.

"It's just not," Evelyn said, shaking her head, "how I pictured your first night here. Petra was going to make filet mignons. We were going to have a nice dinner, the whole family together, not take-out in the kitchen after coming home from an emergency room. . . ."

I looked sympathetically at my aunt's tilted head. Poor Aunt Evelyn. Now she was starting to know how my mother must feel all the time. About me.

I said, with feeling, "I'm sorry."

Evelyn's head popped up again. "What?" she said. "Sorry? What are you sorry for? It's not *your* fault—"

Except, of course, that it was. I'd known what I was doing. I'd known the bike would hit me, and not Zach.

But I'd also known that the blow wouldn't be nearly as bad as it would have been, if it had been Zach. Because I'd been expecting it, and he hadn't.

Why else had the geraniums looked so red?

But of course I didn't say that out loud. Because I'd

learned a long time ago that saying things like that out loud only led to questions I was much better off not answering.

"Knock-knock." Uncle Ted's voice came floating through the closed bedroom door. "Can we come in?"

Tory got up and opened the door. In the hallway stood my uncle Ted, five-year-old Alice in his arms, and ten-year-old Teddy Jr. hiding shyly behind one of Ted's legs.

"I've got some people here," Uncle Ted said, "who want to say good night to their cousin Jean before they go to bed."

"Well," Evelyn said, looking worried. "I guess for just a minute. But—"

Alice, the minute her father put her down, took a flying leap toward my bed, waving a sheet of white butcher paper. "Cousin Jinx, Cousin Jinx," she lisped. "Look what I made you!"

"Gently, Alice," Aunt Evelyn cried. "Gently!"

I said, "That's all right," and pulled Alice, who was wearing a flowered nightdress, into bed with me, the way I used to do with Courtney, back when she'd let me, and still do sometimes, with Sarabeth. "Let me see what you made for me."

Alice displayed her painting proudly. "Look," she said. "It's a picture of the day you were born. There's the hospital, see, and there's you, coming out of Aunt Charlotte."

"Wow," I said, wondering just what they teach kindergartners in New York City. "That sure is . . . graphic."

"Their class guinea pig just had babies," Uncle Ted explained apologetically.

"And see there?" Alice pointed at a large black glob of paint. "That's the cloud the lightning came out of, the lightning that blew out all the lights in the hospital right when you were born." Alice leaned back against my arm, looking pleased with herself.

I said, managing what I hoped was a convincingly encouraging smile, "It's a very nice painting, Alice. I'll hang it right there, above the fireplace."

"The fireplace doesn't work," Teddy informed me, loudly, from the end of the bed.

"Jean knows that," Uncle Ted said. "It's getting too warm out for fires, anyway, Teddy."

"I told 'em this was the best room to put you in," Teddy said to me. "On account of the fireplace already being busted. Because whenever you're around, things get broken."

"Theodore Gardiner Junior!" Evelyn cried. "You apologize to your cousin right this minute!"

"Why?" Teddy asked. "You said it yourself, Mom. That's why everybody calls her Jinx."

"I know a certain young man," Uncle Ted said, "who is going off to bed without dessert."

"Why?" Teddy looked perplexed. "You know it's true. Look at what happened today. Her head got broken."

"Okay," Uncle Ted said, taking hold of Teddy's wrist and dragging him from the room. "That's enough visiting with Cousin Jean. Come on, Alice. Let's go see Petra. I think she's got a bedtime story for you two."

Alice pressed her face up against mine. "*I* don't care if things get broke when you're around," she whispered. "I like you, and I'm glad you're here." She kissed me, smelling of clean five-year-old. "Good night."

"Oh, dear," Evelyn said, when the door had closed again. "I don't know quite what to say."

"It's okay," I said, looking down at Alice's picture. "It's all true."

"Oh, don't be ridiculous, Jinx," my aunt said. "Er, Jean. Things do not get broken when you're around. That thing the night you were born was a whaddayoucallit. A tornado, or supercell, or something. And today was just an accident."

"It's okay, Aunt Evelyn," I said. "I don't mind. I really don't."

"Well, I do." Evelyn took the empty mug and stood up. "I'm going to tell the children not to call you Jinx anymore. It's a ridiculous nickname, anyway. After all, you're practically grown up. Now, if you're sure you don't need anything, Tory and I should go away and let you sleep. And you're not to get out of bed until at least ten tomorrow morning, do you understand? The doctor said plenty of rest. Come on, Tory."

But Tory didn't stir from her chair. "I'll be there in a minute, Mom."

Evelyn didn't seem to have heard her. "I guess I better go and call your mother," she muttered, as she went out of the room. "God only knows how I'm going to explain all this to her. She's going to kill me."

When she was sure her mother was out of earshot, Tory softly closed the bedroom door, then leaned on it, and looked at me with those big, kohl-rimmed blue eyes of hers.

"So," she said. "How long have you known?"

I put down the picture Alice had painted for me. It was past nine o'clock, and I really was tired . . . even though I was still on Iowa time, so it was actually earlier than nine. Physically, I *was* fine, just as I'd assured Aunt Evelyn. The bump on my head hardly even hurt— except to the touch.

But the truth was, I felt exhausted. All I wanted to do was go into that beautiful marble bathroom and wash up, then crawl back into my big comfy bed and sleep. That's all. Just sleep.

But now it appeared I was going to have to wait. Because Tory seemed to want to talk.

"How long have I known what?" I asked, hoping my tiredness didn't show in my voice.

"Well, that you're a witch, of course," she said.

CHAPTER SIX

I blinked at her. Tory looked perfectly serious, leaning against the door. She still had on the black minidress, and her makeup was still perfectly arranged. Four hours of sitting in a hard plastic chair in a hospital emergency waiting room had done nothing to mar her perfect beauty.

"A *what*?" My voice broke on the word *what*.

"A witch, of course." Tory smiled tolerantly. "I know you're one, there's no use denying it. One witch always knows another."

I began to believe, not so much from what Tory had said, but from the curiously tense way in which she was holding her body—like our cat Stanley always does back home, when he's getting ready to pounce—that Tory was serious.

Just my luck. It would have been nice if she'd just been joking around.

I said, choosing my words with care, "Tory, I'm sorry, but I'm tired, and I really want to go to sleep. Maybe we could talk about this some other time . . . ?"

It was the wrong thing to say. All of a sudden, Tory was mad.

"Oh," she said, straightening up. "Oh, *that's* how it is, is it? You think you're better than me, because you've been practicing longer, or something? Is that it? Well, let me tell you something, *Jinx*. I happen to be the most powerful witch in my coven. Gretchen and Lindsey? Yeah, they've got nothing on me. They're still doing stupid little love spells—that don't work, by the way. There are people at school who are *afraid* of me, I'm so powerful. What do you have to say to that, Miss High-and-Mighty?"

My mouth fell open.

The thing is, I should have known. I don't know why, when Mom had told Aunt Evelyn about what was happening, and Aunt Evelyn had suggested I come stay in New York for a while, I thought I'd be safe here.

I should have known. I really should have.

"Is this because of what happened this afternoon?" Tory demanded. "The thing with the pot? Are you mad at me because you found out I do drugs?"

I said, still feeling bewildered—betrayed, even, though I don't know why. It's not like Aunt Evelyn could have any idea what her daughter was up to, or surely she'd have put a stop to it—"No, Tory. Honest. I don't care what you do. Well, I mean, I *care*. And I think it's stupid of you to mess around with medication that wasn't prescribed to you—"

"The Ritalin's just to get me through midterms," Tory interrupted. "And the Valium is just . . . well, sometimes I have trouble sleeping. That's all." Tory had crossed the room, and now she sank down onto the bed. "I'm not, like, hard-core into them, or anything. I don't do ecstasy, or cocaine, or anything like that. What, does your coven frown on drug use, or something? God, that is so quaint."

"Tory," I said. I couldn't quite believe this was happening. "I do not belong to a coven, okay? All I want is to be left alone. No offense, but I'm really tired."

Now it was Tory's turn to blink, and she did so owlishly, staring at me as though I were one of those swan faucets in the bathroom that had suddenly begun to speak. Finally, she said, "You really don't know, do you?"

I shook my head. "Know *what*?"

"That you're one of us," Tory said. "You must have suspected. After all, they call you Jinx."

"Yeah, they call me Jinx," I said, with a bitterness I didn't attempt to disguise, "because, like your little brother said, everything I touch gets messed up."

But Tory was shaking her head. "No. No, it doesn't. Not today, it didn't. Jinx, I *watched* you. I was on the phone with my mom, and I came inside, and I saw the whole thing from the living room." Tory's eyes were so

51

bright, they seemed to glow in the soft light from the bedside lamp. "It was like you knew what was going to happen before anybody even did anything. You shoved Zach out of the way BEFORE that bike hit the sidewalk. You couldn't have known that's the direction that messenger was going to turn. But you *did*. Some part of you *did* know—"

"Of course part of me knew," I said frustratedly. "I've had plenty of experience. If I'm around, whatever is the worst possible thing that can happen, *will* happen. Story of my life. I can't *not* mess something up, if there's anything there to mess up."

"You didn't mess anything up, Jinx," Tory said. "You saved someone's *life*. *Zach's* life."

I shook my head again. This was unbelievable. This was what I had come here to get *away* from. And now it was starting up all over again. My cousin Tory—the last person in the world I would have suspected of such a thing—was trying to start it up.

"Look, Tor," I said. "You're making a big deal out of nothing. I didn't—"

"Yes, Jinx. Yes, you did. Zach says so. If you hadn't done what you did, Zach would have been a pavement pancake."

Suddenly, my stomach was hurting more than my head. I said, "Maybe—"

"Jinx, you're just going to have to face it. You have the gift."

My breath froze in my throat. "The . . . the what?"

"The gift," Tory repeated. "Didn't Grandma ever tell you about Branwen?"

I let out a nervous laugh. What else could I do?

"You mean that crazy story about her great-great-grandmother, or whoever?" I tried to sound as scornful as possible. "Come on, Tory. Don't tell me you believe that baloney. That's just a crazy story Grams pulls out when things get dull in her bridge group down in Boca. . . ."

"It's not baloney," Tory said, looking angry. "And it's not a crazy story. Our great-great-great-great-grand-mother Branwen was a practicing witch, back in Wales. And Branwen told her daughter, who told her daughter, who told her daughter, who told Grandma, that *her* daughter's first daughter—it's only the oldest daughters, not the younger ones—would have the gift. The gift of magic. Sometimes it skips a few generations, I guess. Like you have Grandma's red hair, but neither of our moms has it."

My hand went defensively up to my hair, the way it always did when someone mentioned it.

"Tory," I said. "I really don't—"

"Don't you see? Our great-great-great-whatever-grandmother Branwen was talking about *us*. *We're* our grandmother's daughters' first daughter. Or whatever. We're the next generation of witches in the family."

Oh, boy. I took a deep breath. The knot in my stomach

53

had turned into a full-fledged bowling ball.

"No offense, Tory," I said. "But I think you've seen one too many episodes of *Charmed*. Either that, or you're still high from the gazebo."

Tory sighed. "I guess I'll have to prove it to you, won't I?"

I eyed her nervously. "How are you going to do that?"

"Don't worry," she said with a laugh. "I'm not going to make the mattress levitate or anything." She slipped off the bed and went to the door. "It doesn't work like that. Stay here." She stepped out into the hallway.

Great. So now my cousin Tory thinks she's a witch. This was just so . . . typical—of my luck, anyway.

Not knowing what else to do, I picked up the hand mirror and looked at my bruise some more. There was no doubt about it. It was a bruise, not a bump. It was butt-ugly and no way was it going to be gone in time for my first day at my new school. My exclusive new PRIVATE school in Manhattan. The one that, every time I thought about it, made me feel like throwing up.

Oh, well. It's not like I was any beauty queen to begin with. What had Tory's friend Shawn called me? Oh, yeah. Red. Was that what I had to look forward to on Monday? People mocking me because I have red hair and I come from a traditionally rural state? Am I destined to be Cousin Jean from Iowa for the rest of my life?

Well, it's better than being called Jinx. I guess.

Tory came back into the room, carrying a cardboard shoe box. She closed the door behind her, then brought the shoe box to the bed. There was something in the delicate way Tory was handling the box that made the bowling ball in my stomach feel like it was morphing into something even bigger. A basketball, maybe.

"If you open the lid to that box," I said, "and something comes jumping out at me, I swear I'm going to kill you."

"Nothing's going to jump out at you," Tory said. "Don't be an idiot." She sat down and gently removed the lid from the box. I found myself leaning forward, straining to catch a glimpse of what lay amid the white tissue paper, despite the fact that I was pretty sure I didn't want to know.

And then Tory reached into the box and pulled out . . .

. . . a doll.

My insides churned. I was barely able to make it out of bed and to the side of the toilet before every bit of kung pao chicken and spare ribs that I'd eaten an hour earlier came right back up.

How long I knelt there, heaving, I don't know. But when I came out of the bathroom—feeling, I have to admit, a bit better, the basketball-sized jumble of nerves in my stomach had shrunk to the size of an acorn—Tory was still sitting on the side of my bed, the doll in her lap.

I tried to keep my gaze averted from that doll.

"Are you okay?" Tory asked, looking genuinely worried.

I just nodded and crawled back under the covers. The sheets—they were way softer than the ones we have on the beds back home—felt cool and soothing to my skin.

"That was gross," Tory commented.

"I know," I said, my head sinking into the deep, down-filled pillows. "I'm sorry."

"Do you want me to get my mom?" Tory wanted to know.

"No," I said, closing my eyes. "I'll be all right."

"Good," Tory said. "Anyway. About what I was saying . . ."

"Tory," I said.

"Torrance," she corrected me.

"Torrance," I said, my eyes still closed. "Can we do this later?"

"I'll be really quick," Tory said. "Anyway. See this doll?"

I nodded, my eyes still closed. It didn't matter, because I'd gotten a good look at it before my little trip to bow down before the porcelain god. It was one of the most crudely made dolls I had ever seen. Tory had probably sewn it herself. It was stitched together from some flesh-colored material. It had on a white shirt and gray pants, and a red-and-blue-striped tie. There was something familiar about the outfit it was wearing. The strangest thing about the doll was that on top of its head was a weird assortment of what looked like real human hair, some dark brown, and some aggressively black, much like . . .

. . . much like Tory's.

There was pride in Tory's voice when she asked, "Recognize him?"

I had no choice but to open my eyes.

"I don't know . . ." I said. Then I got it. It was wearing a Chapman uniform. "Is that supposed to be Shawn?" I asked, in a small voice.

"No, silly," Tory said, with a laugh. She clearly didn't notice that anything was wrong. With me, I mean. "It's Zach. See the dark hair? I got him to let me give him a trim last month. He thought I was crazy! Then I took some of his hair and mixed it with some of mine, and made this doll. As long as I keep our hair together, he can't fall in love with anybody else. It's a spell, see? A love spell. I got it off the Internet. Cool, huh?"

A love spell. Off the Internet.

For a second I thought I was going to heave again. Fortunately, the wave of nausea passed.

"I thought you were going out with Shawn," I said weakly.

"I am," Tory said. "But I've always had a thing for Zach—God, he's so hot, don't you think? Of course, he's been my neighbor since, like, forever. So for the longest time, he's barely seemed to know I'm alive. As a girl, anyway. I've just been chubby little Tory from next door. But things have been looking up since I discovered magic . . . and since I made this doll. I think he's finally starting to come around."

"He doesn't," I said, thinking about Zach's comment— *I don't like to cop a buzz before dark*—"seem like your type, exactly." At least, not the type this new and—in her opinion, anyway—improved Tory would like.

"Yeah," she admitted. "He's pretty much more into school than he is into partying. But, you know. That's just because he needs me to liven him up. All that will change when I make him mine."

When I make him mine.

I said, closing my eyes again, "I don't think messing around with witchcraft is a good idea, Tory."

"Why not?" Tory asked, genuinely surprised. "It's in our genetic destiny. And it's working, you know. He hasn't been out with anybody else since I made it. And he comes over after school practically every day."

I thought about what Robert and the others had said. It seemed to me that a far more likely reason Zach came over to the Gardiners' every day was not the fact that Tory had made this doll, but the fact that Petra was here.

I didn't say so out loud, however. I just said, "It seems pretty . . . I don't know. Stalkerish."

"Well," Tory sneered. "You would know."

I opened my eyes to shoot her a dirty look, but said nothing. What could I say? She was right.

In more ways than she knew.

"Whatever," Tory said, with a shrug. "Watch this."

Then Tory removed a needle that had been stuck to the inside of the shoe box, and drove it through the doll Zach's head.

"Hey!" I cried, sitting bolt upright in my bed, my heart hammering. "What are you *doing*?"

"Relax," Tory said. "I'm piercing his thoughts. See? Now he can't help but think of me."

I will admit, I half-expected to hear some kind of shrieking from Zach's room in the house next door. Fortunately, I heard only the burbling of the fountain in the garden below, and a police siren from somewhere in the city.

"Jeez," I said. I watched as Tory rotated the needle around in the doll Zach's cotton-stuffed skull. "I wouldn't be so sure it's you he's thinking of. I'd guess he's thinking of taking an Excedrin."

"Zach hasn't been out with anybody else since I made this doll."

"You said that already," I pointed out. Then, reluctantly, since I wasn't sure how Tory would react, I asked, "But has he asked *you* out?"

"Well," Tory said, putting the doll back into the shoe box. "Not exactly. But I told you, he comes over every—"

"—day after school. Yeah, you said that, too." I shook my head. "Look, I'm sorry, Tor. But this . . . this witch thing? It's not a good idea. Trust me on this. Okay?"

"It's not a *witch thing*," Tory said. "And it's not an *idea*. It's a fact. I'm a witch. You are, too, probably, being a first daughter."

The acorn in my stomach turned into an orange.

"Tory," I said. "I mean, Torrance. I'm serious. Can we talk about this some other time? Because I really don't feel too good."

Tory put the lid back onto the box. "If you're feeling anything, it can only be relief. That at last, you're not alone." Tory leaned forward and laid a hand over mine.

"You're not a freak, Jinx."

If only she knew.

"Gosh," I said. "Thanks. That's . . . comforting."

"I realize it's a lot to digest all at once," Tory went on. "And I'll admit, it was a shock to me, too. The fact is, ever since Grandma first told me that story, the last time we all went down to Florida to see her, I thought *I* was the one. The one Branwen was talking about, the grand-daughter her gift would be passed down to. But there's no denying that, after what I saw today, you, Jinx, have the gift as well. And you have to admit, it *is* pretty likely that, after traveling down through so many generations, Branwen's prediction might have gotten a bit garbled. She must have meant Grandma's *daughters' daughters*. Not Grandma's daughter's daughter. Because Grandma has two daughters, and they each have a daughter. So it must be both of us. We're both witches. There can be room for two witches in one generation, right?"

Not waiting for me to answer, Tory went on, "So all you have to do now is learn how to use it. The gift Branwen left for us, I mean. I can totally help you with that. You just have to come to one of our coven meetings. With our powers—yours and mine combined—there's no telling what we'll be able to do. Rule the school, for one thing. But why stop there? God, Jinx. We could *rule the world*."

I said quickly, "No."

Tory looked surprised. "Why not?"

"Because." I took another deep breath. She was going

to be angry. I knew it. But Tory's anger was better than her finding out the truth. "I don't think messing around with magic is such a good thing, you know? I mean, I don't know much about it, but let's just say it really is true—our great-great-whatever-grandmother was a witch, and passed her powers on to us. Is it really fair of us to use them to trap guys? I mean, from what I do know about witchcraft—doesn't it kind of mandate that practitioners use their powers for good instead of evil?"

"How is getting the guy you're crushing on to like you back evil, exactly?" Tory rolled her eyes. "Please. Don't even get me started on that respecting nature, worshiping trees crap—"

It was all I could do to keep from slapping her.

"It isn't crap," I said, keeping my hands to myself, with an effort. "From what I understand, witchcraft is all about using nature—its energy. If you don't respect what you're drawing power from, that power's going to turn on you. And if you're using that power for something negative—like that doll of yours, the basic purpose of which is to rob Zach of his free will to like whoever he wants to like—then negativity is all you're going to get back."

Tory didn't look surprised anymore. Now she looked mad.

Tory's pretty lips had all but disappeared, she was pressing them together so tightly. "Fine," she said. "Fine. I'd hoped you'd be a little more open-minded about all of this. After all, it *is* your heritage. But if you want to be an unsophisticated hick your whole life, that's your prerogative. Just remember, Jinx. We're here, when you change your mind."

She stood up, holding the box containing the doll of Zach, and walked away.

"In fact," she added, when she got to the door. "We're *everywhere*."

Like I didn't already know it.

CHAPTER SEVEN

"Outta my way."

I veered to the left of the path, only to hear someone else behind me bark, "Hey, move it!"

I hurriedly stepped out of the way, and the runners passed me by. They were all passing me by. I know I'm not the world's most athletic person, or anything, but this was ridiculous.

The whole thing was ridiculous, actually. My school system back home in Iowa requires only one year of high school physical education, and I'd done mine freshman year.

At the Chapman School, it turns out, only the senior class is exempt from P.E. Which is great—obesity is rampant in America, it's important to stay fit, and all of that.

But that's how I now found myself, my first day at my new school, slogging along the dirt path around the Central Park reservoir—because the Chapman School does not have a gym, and so they hold their physical education classes in the world's most famous park—in a white T-shirt and a pair of royal blue running shorts that were, in my opinion, embarrassingly short.

As if it's not bad enough that I'm the world's slowest runner. I have to look stupid doing it, too.

So typical of my luck.

"Move over," someone panted behind me. So I did. This time, it was a fleet-footed blond girl who jogged past. I watched her bobbing ponytail as it disappeared around a gentle bend in the trail, and wondered what it was about me that had already made me such a social outcast at the Chapman School.

At first I thought it couldn't be my clothes that were making me such a pariah, since everyone at Chapman has to wear a uniform.

Then I realized it could be my jewelry—or lack thereof. Most of the girls in my classes—including the blonde who'd just passed me—had diamond studs in their ears, some of them the size of my pinky nails. I highly doubted they were cubic zirconium.

And their watches . . . I had been amazed to learn that Tory's was a Gucci. Chanelle owned a Rolex. Nobody at Chapman seems to have ever heard of Swatch or Timex.

And apparently loafers from Nine West are not considered appropriate footwear for a Chapman sophomore. Even though the only difference I could detect between my shoes and Tory's Ferragamos was about four hundred dollars, there's something wrong with mine, whereas Tory's are acceptable.

Apparently the fact that my shoes are from the wrong place, and I own no expensive jewelry, coupled with the giant bruise on my forehead—always an attractive accessory—and my complete inability to enter or exit a classroom without either tripping over or banging into someone or something were largely to thank for my loser status.

Even this far from home, it turned out, I could not escape my nickname, since Tory scathingly called me by it when I dropped a can of soda—which promptly exploded—at lunch in the cafeteria my very first day, and everyone, since then, had followed her example by calling me Jinx.

Jinx. I'm always going to be Jinx.

You're not a hundred-dollar bill, Grandma was fond of telling us kids during her frequent visits from her retirement community in the Sunshine State. *Not everybody's going to like you.*

Wasn't that the understatement of the year. Like it wasn't hard enough being a preacher's daughter. I mean, people either expect you to be a priss, or totally slutty, like Lori Singer's character from the movie *Footloose*.

And it was like people could just . . . tell. About the preacher's daughter thing. Maybe it really was my country-fresh looks. Maybe it was the violin—I'd joined the school's orchestra, the only class where I remotely seemed to fit in . . . although waves had been made when I scored second chair straight off the bat.

Like it's my fault I'm a geek who actually enjoys practicing.

Or maybe it was my unfamiliarity with Kanye West and *The Hills* and other music and shows we aren't allowed to listen to or watch in my house, because of my younger siblings.

Whatever it was—all of the above or something I hadn't even considered yet—it was like someone had rubber-stamped OUTCAST across my forehead, and most of the student population at Chapman responded accordingly.

But at least, out here in the wilds of Central Park, there weren't a whole lot of people to see me mess up, trip over a tree root as I ran, or whatever. Of course, it was just my luck that I'd started school on the first day of the Presidential Fitness test, part of which entailed a timed run. I had really thought the P.E. instructor was joking when he'd pointed at the reservoir—which is more like a lake, in my opinion—and informed us that we were to run around it twice.

Was he kidding?

Apparently not, since the rest of the class—with so many people, and all dressed the same, and me so shy, unwilling to meet anyone's gaze, I hadn't even been able to get a good look at any of them to size up the competition, so to speak—took off, pounding along the dirt trail.

I'd had to hurry to catch up.

Still, it wasn't completely unpleasant. It was weird to be in so much wilderness—with trees so thick all around me—and yet still be able to see skyscrapers towering above the top branches.

And there were other people on the trail besides the ones from my class. There were tourists, enjoying a stroll in the park with their fanny packs and cameras, and groups of little school kids, visiting with their teachers on their way to the American Museum of Natural History, and even horseback riders, in their jodhpurs and black helmets, trotting right alongside the joggers.

It was actually all kind of cool.

Well, except for the running part.

And then a guy's voice from behind me said, "Hey."

Thinking it was someone else who wanted me to move over—even though I was as far over on the trail as I could get without going off it—I looked back, annoyed . . .

And stumbled over a root.

"Whoa." The runner slowed and bent over. "You all right, Cousin Jean from Iowa?"

I hadn't fallen—at least. I'd stumbled, but I hadn't fallen flat on my face, or even hurt myself, for once. I straightened and said, hoping he couldn't see how hard my heart was thumping (and not just from the exercise) while at the same time trying not to smile too broadly—"Hi, Zach."

He grinned down at me. Like me, he was dressed in a white T-shirt. But unlike me, his royal blue shorts didn't look too short at all. They looked just right.

More than all right. They looked *great.*

"I didn't know you were in this class," I said. Then I knit my brow. "*Why* are you in this class? I thought you were a junior."

Zach shrugged. "Chapman requires three years of P.E. So here I am."

"Oh," I said intelligently.

Some runners came tearing around the bend. Zach grabbed me by the arm and pulled me off the path, into some scrubby brush.

"Jeez," he said, looking after the runners, clearly annoyed. "What do they think this is, the Olympics?"

I said, "Well . . ." I couldn't think of anything else to say. "We better join them, I guess, or the president will be disappointed in our lack of fitness."

Zach looked at his watch. I couldn't tell if it was a Rolex, like everyone else's at Chapman. But it looked pretty impressive.

"Tell you what," he said. "I don't actually believe the president cares about my level of fitness. Let's get out of here."

I looked back at the path. "But if we don't finish our run . . ."

"Oh, we will," Zach said, still grinning. "We'll come huffing and puffing along right with the best of them. Only I know a shortcut. . . ."

I looked at the dirt trail, and then back at Zach. I have never in my life skipped a class. I mean, I'm a preacher's daughter.

But it kind of hit me then: Mom wasn't exactly around.

Fortunately the knot in my stomach—which had been growing and shrinking all day, depending on the circumstances—was apparently dormant just then . . . though whether because of Zach's presence, or in spite of it, I had no idea.

So I said, "Well, all right. If you promise we won't get in trouble. I don't want to get in trouble my first day."

He held up three fingers. "Scout's honor."

I smiled. "You were never a Boy Scout. I bet they don't even *have* Boy Scouts in New York."

He said, "Well, they probably do, but you're right. I never was one."

Zach's shortcut took us, instead of deeper into the wilds of the park, as I'd been afraid it might, onto a paved sidewalk which wasn't exactly crowded with people, but which had enough ice cream vendors and tourists hanging around it to make me feel at ease. In fact, Zach strolled right up to one of the ice cream vendors, then turned to ask me, "What'll it be?"

I stooped to look at the photographs on the side of the cart. I didn't recognize a lot of the cones. Even the *ice cream* in New York is different.

"Gee," I said, looking at a massive red, white, and blue ice pop. "What's *that* one?"

"Two Jumbo Jetstars," Zach said to the vendor. To me,

he said, "Otherwise known as Rockets. I can't believe you've never had one before. What do they eat back in Iowa, anyway? Potato cones?"

Offended on behalf of my state, I said indignantly, "That's Idaho. And there's lots of good ice cream in Iowa. Like cherry-dipped cones."

Zach shrugged. "Bet you guys don't have gelato."

"We most certainly do."

"And I know what a cherry dip is. I also know it's disgusting, and certainly nothing I'd ever brag about ingesting." The vendor handed Zach two pops, and Zach passed him a five-dollar bill he pulled out from his gym sock. Which is when I realized I had no cash on me.

"My treat," Zach said, when I mentioned this. Then he presented my Jumbo Jetstar with a gallant flourish. "It's the least I can do, considering you saved my life. If these were ancient times, I think I'd owe you eternal servitude, or something."

I felt myself turning as red as the top third of the ice pop I held. "I didn't save your life," I said.

"Yeah?" Zach looked amused. "Suit yourself, then. How do you like your Rocket?"

It tasted like every other ice pop I'd had in my life, but I said, to be polite, "It's very good."

"Told you."

The ice pop was actually cooling me off a little. It was hot for April, and now that we'd left the shade of the trees, the sun beat down on us. The warm weather had brought out Rollerbladers, as well as ice cream vendors and nannies pushing baby strollers. I even saw a few people sunbathing.

"So," Zach said, as we strolled. "Your bruise looks better."

I put a hand to it self-consciously. He was only being nice, of course. The bruise, if anything, looked worse than ever. Zach had seen it the day before, when he and his parents had come over to the Gardiners' to see how I was doing. To my complete and utter mortification, they'd brought with them two dozen pink roses which they'd presented to me with their thanks for what they perceived that I'd done for Zach.

I had tried to be gracious, the way my mom would have wanted me to be. But it was hard. I mean, everyone—not just Tory—thought I'd done this huge, noble thing, thrusting myself in the path of this out-of-control bicyclist. When really, all I'd done was just been my typical luckless self. The whole time Zach and his parents had been there, I'd been unable to keep from wishing that a hole would open up in the Gardiners' parquet floor and swallow me alive. Zach's parents were both supersmart, his father an entertainment lawyer, his mother a tax lawyer, and they were certainly very nice people.

But I would have infinitely preferred it if they'd stayed home. I'm hardly the world's most sociable person, and I had felt extremely uncomfortable being the focus of so much attention.

It was too bad, in fact, that it had been me, and not Tory, who'd been there when the bike messenger had nearly hit Zach. Had Tory, and not me, saved Zach, she would have enjoyed all the fuss, the roses, the concern. Instead, Tory had been forced to experience it all second-hand, leaning against the wall with one fishnetted knee propped up, a tiny, catlike smile on her lips, watching as I uncomfortably replied to Zach's parents' polite attempts at conversation.

Zach, for his part, had sat on the white couch in the Gardiners' den with a Coke cradled between his hands, contributing little, but smiling quite a lot. Later, Tory had pointed out that Zach had been staring the whole time at her knee, the one she'd propped up. Because, you know, he wants her so badly, or something.

I had a little different impression—that Zach had been staring at *me*. Because every time I'd looked up, his gaze had seemed to meet mine.

I didn't mention this to Tory, however. And probably, I was wrong, and he *had* been looking at Tory's knee.

Still, everyone had had plenty of opportunity to look at my bruise, analyze its size and color, and estimate how long it would be before it went away. I had almost considered packing up and going back to Iowa (not really, of course).

But it did make me miss my own family, who take my absurd brushes with fate (and things like bike messengers) in stride. Even reading and replying to several e-mails from my best friend, Stacy, from the laptop

Uncle Ted had loaned me later that evening hadn't helped.

But then I remembered that being presented with two dozen roses by the parents of a boy I (might as well admit it) was crushing on—and whom I knew would never like me back because of his own crush on a very cute German au pair—was infinitely better than what was going on at home.

Now, I looked down at my Jumbo Jetstar (wishing more than ever that, all those months ago, I had made a very different choice), and said, "Thanks."

"What I haven't quite figured out yet," Zach said, as we strolled past a pond in which people—even some grown men—were sailing little model boats, "is why everybody in your family calls you Jinx."

I sighed. "I would think it would be perfectly obvious, after what happened. I'm a bad luck magnet. In fact, since birth, wherever I am . . . well, things always seem to go screwy." I told him about the supercell that struck the very moment I'd been born, and the people who'd had to be airlifted to the hospital the next county over, due to all the power going off.

"The doctor who delivered me joked that they should name me Jinx, not Jean," I went on. "And everyone thought that was real funny, so the name stuck. Unfortunately."

Zach shrugged. "Well, that's not so bad. My dad has a client who was born with a lot of spit in her mouth, so everybody calls her Bubbles. That would be worse."

I said, "I guess so."

But I kind of doubt that Bubbles has gone through the rest of her life with saliva bubbling out of her mouth, whereas my streak of bad luck had still not let up, not for sixteen years.

Which reminded me of something I had meant to ask Zach, if I ever ran into him alone again.

"About my cousin Tory," I began tentatively. Because, of course, although I knew how Tory felt about *him*, I didn't know how Zach felt about Tory. I remembered how surprised he'd looked when Robert had mentioned his crush on Petra . . . and Tory's crush on him.

"Yeeesss?" He stretched the word out so that it had multiple syllables.

"Does she do . . . um, drugs . . . a lot? I mean, like, is there a problem? Or is it just a recreational thing? Not that I'm going to say anything to her parents," I hastened to add. The other bad thing about being a preacher's daughter is that everyone automatically assumes you're a narc. "But if it's serious—"

"Tough being the preacher's daughter," Zach said, tossing a penny he'd found into the pond we were standing near. "Isn't it?"

Whoa. I flushed. It was like he'd read my mind.

"Yeah," I said, feeling my heartstrings twang again. Calm down, Jean. He's in love with Petra, with whom you could never compete. Even if you wanted to. Which you don't, because she's your friend. "It is, sometimes."

"Thought as much. Don't tell anyone—it'll destroy my street cred—but *Seventh Heaven* was my favorite show when I was a kid." He winked.

I laughed. I liked how it appeared that when I was with him, the knot in my stomach seemed to go away. "It's not actually like that," I said. "At least, not that bad. I just . . . I'm worried about her, is all."

"Most of what your cousin Tory says and does," Zach said, "she says and does to get attention. Your aunt and uncle are busy people, and Tory's a bit of a drama queen, in case you didn't notice. I think she feels like she has to go to extremes to get noticed. Like with this witch stuff."

The pain in my stomach returned, with a vengeance. Wow. So much for it going away when Zach was around.

"Oh," I said, my heartstrings banging—not twanging. And not in a good way. "You know about that?"

"Are you kidding? I think Tory's made sure the whole school knows. Her and that coven of hers. They actually brought a cauldron to school one time," he went on, "to do their witchy little spells in the caf. Only they set off the smoke alarm. Principal Baldwin was *pissed*. Tory tried to make this big stink about how he was preventing her from practicing her religion. Like witchcraft is a religion."

"Actually," I said, stung by his tone, "it can be. But you shouldn't get what Tory and her friends are doing—playing at being witches—and real witchcraft mixed up. Real witches don't cast spells to get attention, but because it gives them actual spiritual fulfillment. And witchcraft, if it's done properly, is more about giving thanks—and showing appreciation—for nature than it is about trying to bend it to someone's will or . . . or make things magically appear."

"Don't tell me," he said, sounding disapproving, "you're one of them, too."

"I'm not," I hastened to assure him. "But one of the side effects of being a preacher's daughter is an interest in spiritual practices. *All* spiritual practices. I can tell you all about shamanism, too, if you want."

"Rain check on that," Zach said. "I guess this means I'll have to take your word for it on the spiritual thing. Still, I can't help thinking your cousin isn't into this witch stuff for any New Age, crunchy-granola reason, but because it's the hot new thing in her social set."

"I think it goes a little deeper than that for Tory," I said, thinking of how angry she'd gotten with me during our conversation about our ancestress, Branwen, my first night in New York. "But I'm relieved you don't seem to think she has a problem. With drugs, I mean."

"Honestly, I think Tory's too smart ever to get herself in over her head that way. I think a lot of what you saw in the gazebo the other day was just . . . well, showing off."

For him. He didn't say so, but who else could Tory have been showing off for?

The question was, did he know it?

Thinking it might be best to change the subject, since the last thing I wanted to do was get accused by Tory of talking about her behind her back—and these things do have a way of getting back to people—I asked, "So where did you spend your year abroad?"

Zach's descriptions of the sights and sounds of Florence, Italy, took us all the way up to Fifth and Eighty-ninth, where Coach Winthrop, the P.E. instructor, was waiting with his stopwatch. We threw our ice pop sticks away—I had only managed to get down to the white part of my Rocket, and not even sampled the blue—and did a few stretches to limber up for our big finish. Then, crouching behind some bushes, we waited until a herd of royal-blue-shorts-wearing runners came our way, then came bursting out to join them . . .

. . . and thundered toward Coach Winthrop and his stopwatch, panting as hard as if we'd just run ten miles, and not just a tiny fraction of one.

"Excellent, Rosen," the coach said, throwing a towel in Zach's direction. "You cut a whole minute from your sophomore year's time."

I couldn't hold back a fit of giggles any longer, especially when Zach said somberly, slinging the towel around his neck, "Thanks, Coach. I've been training pretty hard."

Later, as we were filing back into school, Zach found me in the crowd of girls trying to get into the girls' locker room to shower and change, and asked, "Hey, Jean, have you tried souvlaki yet?"

"No." I felt myself turning red, because, of course,

the other girls turned to see who he was talking to.

"Oh, man," Zach said, grinning mysteriously. "Tomorrow, we try the souvlaki. Are you in for a treat." Then without another word, he ducked into the boys' locker room.

Whoa. So Zach was planning on taking me for souvlaki tomorrow during class.

Which was kind of like a date.

Well, okay, maybe not, because he was probably only doing it to make up for that whole thing where I saved his life.

But still.

It wasn't until I was freshly showered and headed for my next class in a dreamy daze that I remembered that Zach wasn't exactly a free man. I mean, if the rumors were true, he was in love with Petra . . .

. . . and my cousin was madly in love with him.

Madly enough in love with him to make a doll of him, and stick it with pins.

Which meant, if I did anything to displease her—such as go for souvlaki with the guy she liked—there was nothing to keep her from doing the same thing to me.

And it wouldn't be my thoughts she'd be piercing, I was pretty sure.

And yet, remembering the way Zach's green eyes had laughed into mine at the finish line in P.E. that day, I found I didn't even care. I didn't care that Tory loved him. And I didn't care that he, in turn, loved Petra.

That's how far gone I already was.

You would think, given my lifetime of experience, I'd have recognized the warning signs.

But that just goes to show how really rotten my luck is, after all.

CHAPTER EIGHT

It was as I was pouring Mouche's used-up cat litter into a trash bag that I saw it.

Chores. They were a big deal around the Gardiner household. Not because there were so many of them. It was because there were so few. Thanks to Petra, the au pair, and Marta, the housekeeper, and Jorge, the gardener, there wasn't a whole lot left for us kids to do around the brownstone.

But Aunt Evelyn and Uncle Ted believed as strongly as my parents did that children needed to learn responsibility, so a few days after my arrival—once my bruise had had a chance to die down—there'd been some discussion as to what my "chore" would be.

"She can't have my job," Teddy had declared. We'd been eating the filet mignon Petra had promised to cook the night of my arrival . . . just a few nights late. "I'm in charge of emptying the dishwasher when Marta's not here, and feeding the koi. And I *like* my jobs."

"She can have my jobs," Tory muttered. She had decided just that morning that she was a vegetarian, and had forced Petra to prepare her tofu instead of filet mignon. And it looked to me like she was regretting that decision, if the way she was gazing at my steak was any indication. "Loading the dishwasher, and the cat box. I don't know why *I* have to clean the cat box every day."

Aunt Evelyn had looked at Tory darkly. "Because you're the one who wanted a cat," she pointed out. "You told us you'd take full responsibility for her."

Tory rolled her eyes. "That cat," she said, "is the most ungrateful animal I've ever seen. She sleeps with *Alice* every night, even though *I'm* the one who feeds her and cleans her box."

Alice, who was eating her filet mignon hamburger-style, between two slices of white bread and smothered in ketchup, said indignantly, "Maybe if you didn't scream at Mouche all the time for getting hair all over your black clothes, she'd want to sleep with you more."

Tory rolled her eyes again and said, "Just give Jinx cat box duty."

Aunt Evelyn didn't approve of the new arrangement—of me taking over Tory's job of monitoring Mouche's litter box—but that's what happened. I also volunteered to watch Teddy and Alice on the one afternoon when Petra's class schedule did not allow her to get back to the city in time to do so, a chore formerly performed by Marta . . . I guess since no one had ever been able to get Tory to do it. Not even her own parents.

But then, I didn't exactly mind. I genuinely liked my younger cousins, because they reminded me of my own brothers and sisters, whom I was missing much more than I ever thought I would—thirteen-year-old aspiring model Courtney; ten-year-old baseball fanatic Jeremy; seven-year-old Sarabeth, obsessed with Bratz; and especially four-year-old Henry, the baby of the family.

Having chores to perform, just like the ones I'd left behind, made me feel less lonely and more like I belonged to the Gardiner family, which, in turn, made me miss my own less.

Still, when weekly allowance day rolled around, and Aunt Evelyn presented me with a brand-new fifty-dollar bill, I knew I wasn't back in Iowa anymore.

Staring down at it, I asked, "What's this for?" thinking she must want change back.

"Your allowance." Aunt Evelyn passed Tory an identical bill. Teddy and Alice, whose financial needs were apparently deemed less dire, received a twenty and a ten, respectively.

"But . . ." I stared down at the bill. Fifty dollars? For scooping Mouche's box and picking the kids up after school once a week? "I can't take this. You're already paying my tuition for school and letting me stay here and everything—"

I suspected the Gardiners had done more than this, even. I couldn't be sure, but I gathered, from things I heard around school, that not just anyone was admitted to Chapman. There was a wait list, one that I had apparently jumped to the head of, due to a "donation" the Gardiners had made on my behalf. I didn't know if my parents were aware of this, but I certainly was, and it made me more conscious than ever of just how much I owed the Gardiners. Especially since I'd brought the reason for my needing to transfer to Chapman on myself.

I did *not* deserve one more *cent* of their money.

But they apparently felt differently.

"Honestly, Jean," Aunt Evelyn said, "I owe you at least as much for looking after Teddy and Alice every Wednesday. Any babysitter in Manhattan would have charged much more."

"Yes, but . . ." I mean, I'd been looking after my own siblings, free of charge, for my entire life. "Really, I don't think—"

"God, Jinx." Tory shook her head at me in disbelief. "Are you crazy? Just take it."

"I agree," Aunt Evelyn said. "Take the money, Jean. I'm sure this weekend you'll want to go to the movies or something with some of your new friends from school. Enjoy yourself. You deserve it."

I didn't exactly point out that I had no new friends from school. Oh, there were the kids from orchestra, who liked me well enough, once they got over an outsider scoring second chair violin her first day. If you can play an instrument, you'll always fit in with the orchestra crowd.

And there was Chanelle, whom I sat next to at lunch.

But she was Tory's friend, really—although she took no part in Tory and Gretchen and Lindsey's "coven" talk, and seemed to be there, really, just because that's where her boyfriend, Robert, sat with Shawn. Tory let me sit there, too, but never without giving the impression that by allowing me to do so, she was granting me this humongous favor. I knew she'd have preferred for me to sit with the orchestra crowd, instead. *I* would have preferred to sit with them, too.

But I couldn't figure out a way to do it that wouldn't cause Tory to make some sarcastic comment. Because even though I knew she didn't want me there, I knew she'd like it even less if I deserted her. She hadn't exactly been Ms. Friendly since the whole Branwen conversation.

Still, ill-gotten as I felt it was, I found a use for my sudden financial windfall the first day I changed out the litter in Mouche's box.

The Gardiners favored clumping cat litter, which is easy to clean, since all you have to do is sift through it with a little slotted shovel.

But either the litter was inferior, or Tory hadn't changed it in a very long time, because no matter how thoroughly I scooped it, it still smelled . . . a lot. The ammonia-like odor of cat urine literally filled the utility room in which the box sat. I felt sorry for Marta, who had to use the utility room every time she did the laundry.

So I found an unopened container of litter, and

decided to give Mouche a fresh new supply, after dumping out the old.

I didn't understand what I was looking at, at first. I thought it had to be a mistake. Then I saw the tape, and realized it wasn't a mistake. I dropped the empty litter box like it had caught on fire.

Because even though I'd dumped out all the old litter, the box wasn't empty. Not completely. Taped to the bottom of it, previously hidden under several inches of old, smelly cat litter, was a photograph. A photograph that I could see, in spite of the fact that it was scratched up and considerably faded, was of Petra.

I couldn't believe it. I really couldn't believe it. Because I knew who had put that photo there.

I also knew why.

I just couldn't believe anyone—*anyone*—would be so mean.

Maybe, I thought, as I carefully peeled the photo up from the bottom of the box, Tory hadn't known what she was doing. She *couldn't* have known. *No one* who knew what something like that could do to someone would ever try it . . . not even on her worst enemy—

Oh, right. Who was I kidding? Tory had known *exactly* what she was doing.

Which was why I knew I had no choice but to try to stop her . . . by whatever means necessary.

Even if it meant breaking my word.

And okay, it had only been a promise to myself.

But sometimes, those are the hardest ones to break.

I found what I needed online . . . a store—an actual *store*—that carried what I was looking for. Such a store, in Hancock, would surely have been shut down by outraged citizens.

In New York, however, that was apparently not a concern.

The store, which was in the East Village, closed at seven. I had two hours to figure out how to get down there.

The subway was the most logical choice, but since I'd never ridden on the New York subway, the thought of doing so filled me with terror.

The problem was, what might happen if I *didn't* make the trip filled me with even more terror . . . just for different reasons.

So I fished a subway map out of a drawer in the kitchen, where I knew Aunt Evelyn kept such things, and left the house, studying the map carefully as I walked.

I had gone approximately three steps before someone reached out and crumpled the map up in front of me. My heart thumping, I looked up . . .

. . . and nearly crumpled up myself when I saw it was Zach Rosen.

"Do not," he said, "walk down the streets of New York City with your head buried in a subway map. People will know you're from out of town, and will try to take advantage of you."

After having spent every fifth period of that entire

week shirking the Presidential Fitness Test with him, and instead exploring the delicacies offered by what Zach calls the Umbrella Cafés of Central Park, including the mysterious—and delicious—souvlaki, I felt comfortable enough to wail, "I have to go to the East Village. Do you know which subway I should take?"

Zach, who'd slung off his backpack and was obviously just returning from somewhere, nevertheless shouldered it again and said, "Let's go."

Okay, THAT was not an answer I'd anticipated.

"No," I said, appalled. Because he was the last person I wanted to know where I was going. Not because I was still crushing on him . . . I was, of course, even though I knew it was completely futile. Just yesterday, in fact, I had gotten Zach to admit he was in love with Petra. The conversation—which had taken place in the Gardiners' kitchen after school, where I had found him recovering from a game of catch he and Teddy had been having in front of the brownstone—had gone like this:

Me (summoning all my courage, after Petra had finally left the room with Teddy, in order to supervise the washing of his exceptionally grubby hands before letting him sample cookies from a batch she'd just made): "So is it true you're in love with Petra?"

Zach (choking on a cookie): "What makes you think that?"

Me: "Because Robert said that day I first met you that that's the only reason you hang around here."

Zach: "And Robert, as we know, is a consummate authority on all things, having such keen perception that is in no way compromised by mind-altering substances."

Me (heartstrings twanging): "So you're saying Robert is wrong? You never liked Petra?"

Zach: "I will admit there was a time when I found Petra quite fetching."

Me (not even jealous because Petra really *is* fetching, plus kindhearted and a great cook): "But she has a boyfriend."

Zach: "I know. I've met him. Willem. He's very cool."

Me: "But you still keep hanging around."

Zach (gets up): "Does my hanging around bother you? Because I can leave."

Me (panicking): "No! I just . . . you know. I just wonder why you still hang around. If you know she has a boyfriend."

Zach (holding up a cookie): "Aren't the plentiful baked goods around here excuse enough?"

Me: "Admit it. You still think you have a chance with her."

Zach: "Is there someone in this house with whom you think I'd have a better chance?"

Me (thinking of Tory, with whom he'd definitely have a better chance, but whom he should definitely steer clear of, considering that doll): "I guess not."

Zach (looking amused): "Well, then."

The thing is, I didn't even mind about his loving Petra. Because for one thing, it gave us plenty to talk about—not that we ever seemed to fall short in that capacity, since we seemed to share the same opinion on a lot of things, such as politics, food, music (although Zach wasn't actually all that familiar with classical), a hatred for organized sports of any kind, and the deplorable state into which the show *7th Heaven* had sunk ever since Jessica Biel left it as a full-time cast member.

But on the rare occasions when there was a lull in conversation, I could always mention something Petra-related—that maybe if Zach took German lessons, he could surprise her by asking her how she was doing in her native language, or something like that. Personally, I think he really appreciated my help in his pursuit of her.

And I, in turn, really appreciated that I didn't have to worry about how I looked or acted around him. It didn't matter that my Chapman School shorts were so ugly, or that I walked into the paths of Rollerbladers almost daily and had to be pulled to safety by him. Because he wasn't interested in me that way. We were just friends. When I was with Zach, I could forget all the horrible things I was running away from, and just relax. My stomach didn't even hurt when I was with him . . . well, unless I happened to find my mind straying, and wondering what might happen if Petra somehow disappeared from the picture, and Zach—miracle of miracles—ever *did* happen to think of me as more than a friend.

That's when my stomach would seize up. Because, of course, he'd made it clear how he felt about witches and witchcraft, and there was . . .

Well. My past.

And then there was Tory.

But I tried to talk about her to him as little as possible. I still didn't know if he knew how much she liked him—or if, witch thing aside, he could ever like her back. I couldn't see how, actually, any guy *wouldn't* be flattered to learn that a girl as pretty as Tory liked him.

Still, while it was true that Zach and I were friends, we weren't good enough friends for us to discuss Tory's crush on him—and *definitely* not good enough friends to let him know where I was headed on the subway that day.

"No, you don't have to come with me," I said hastily. "Can you just tell me how I would get to Ninth Street between Second and First Avenues?"

But he just shook his head. "Nuh-uh. You're not going all the way down there alone. People call you Jinx for a reason, right? God only knows what kind of disasters you might walk into."

"But—"

"If you think I'm letting you go to the East Village by yourself, you're nuts." He took hold of my arm, and swung me around. "For one thing, I still owe you eternal servitude for saving my life, remember? And for another, the subway station's that way, stupid. Let's go."

There isn't anything in the least romantic about being called stupid. Really. Especially since I knew there was no way Zach would ever be interested in a red-haired, violin-playing preacher's daughter when there was the remotest chance he could have gorgeous, physical-therapist-in-training Petra.

So why did I feel so ridiculously happy, all the way downtown? I had forgotten all about my anger at Tory—and my disgust with myself, for going back on my word, as I knew I was about to do. I hardly noticed the rush-hour hordes into which we threw ourselves as we boarded the train, and didn't pay the least bit of attention to the men who begged for quarters in the car, or the signs warning passengers to watch their wallets, or the cops on the platforms with their bomb-sniffing dogs . . . all of which might have terrified me—if I hadn't been with Zach.

Oh, let's face it. Sure, he liked another girl. But I was gone anyway. He'd had me at *I like seals.*

But when we finally reached East Ninth Street between Second and First Avenues, I realized that Zach really *was* going to think I was stupid—or at least seriously deranged—when he saw the kind of store into which I was headed.

I slowed my pace as we approached it. I could see the sign, cut into the shape of a crescent moon, hanging above a black awning. ENCHANTMENTS, it said. What was I going to say when he asked—as he undoubtedly would—why I was going to a store that specialized in . . .

well . . . witch paraphernalia?

Zach was telling me about a documentary he'd seen the night before about a team of plastic surgeons who go to Third World countries to perform free corrective surgery on kids with cleft palates and stuff. Zach is very into documentaries. He wants to study film when he gets to NYU, and make documentaries about arctic wildlife, such as seals, and how we are destroying their habitats. He'd even taken me to see his seals—the ones at the Central Park Zoo. He knows all of their names, too, and can tell them apart.

I listened to his summary about the documentary with only half an ear. I was trying to tell myself that Zach wasn't going to care about the store I was going into. Really, I was blowing the whole thing out of proportion. We're friends. Friends don't care what kind of books their friends read. Right?

But, just as I'd suspected would happen, Zach dried up when I stopped in front of the store. It didn't help any that there were crystals and tarot cards in the display window, arranged on a bunch of black velvet. Nor did it help that, as we stood there, the door opened, and two women dressed all in black, their hair dyed the same way Tory's was, came out, carrying paper bags and chattering cheerfully.

"*This* is where you wanted to go?" Zach asked, his dark eyebrows raised. Disapprovingly, just as I'd suspected.

"I . . ." I had spent most of the walk down Ninth Street concocting a story I hoped would sound convincing. "I have to get something for my little sister—"

"Courtney?" he asked. "Or Sarabeth?"

"Courtney," I said, trying to ignore a rush of pleasure that he'd remembered my sister's name. Both my sisters' names! I'd only told him a million stories about them. I couldn't believe he'd actually been listening. "Her birthday is coming up, and I thought she'd like this, plus I don't think you can find a book like it in Iowa."

Wait. Did that sound as lame to him as it did to me?

But all Zach said was, "Ever heard of Barnes and Noble? There's one only a couple blocks away from where we live," in an amused voice. "We didn't have to come all the way down here, you know."

"Blessed be," said the pretty, dark-haired woman behind the counter, as we came into the store.

"Um," I said, blushing. Because of what Zach must be thinking—that she was a New Age, crunchy-granola type. "Thanks."

I hurried past the counter, heading blindly for the back, where I'd glimpsed some bookshelves. Still, I couldn't help noticing that the store was crammed with herbs and candles, amulets and lunar calendars. A black cat lay across one shelf, her tail twitching slowly back and forth as she watched me approach. Around her neck was a turquoise collar with a pentacle hanging from it where a bell might have been on a normal, non-witch cat.

93

I reached for the book I was looking for—not one of the big, glossy-covered ones, filled with photos and chapters called "Love Spells," which were the kind Tory and her friends might have picked up, but a small, pictureless, paper-bound thing—*not* available at any chain bookstore—and flipped to the back, scanning the index. Zach, meanwhile, was wandering around, picking things up and examining them curiously. When he got to the cat, he stopped and scratched it under the chin. The cat began to purr, so loudly that I could hear it halfway across the store.

So he liked cats, too. Au pairs, *7th Heaven*, seals, kids . . . and cats. Could this guy possibly get any cuter?

A bell tinkled, and two girls strolled into the store. Two girls wearing Chapman School uniforms. Two girls I, unfortunately, recognized.

The knot in my stomach, which had been visiting less and less lately, suddenly made its presence known.

The pretty saleslady behind the counter said, "Blessed be," to her two new customers.

And Gretchen and Lindsey said, "Blessed be," back to her, Lindsey giggling the whole time.

"How old is Courtney turning, anyway?" Zach, appearing from behind a rack of herbs, wanted to know. "Twelve?"

I jumped, and said automatically, "Fourteen."

I'd stopped scanning the book's index. I'd found what I was looking for.

But how was I going to buy it without Gretchen and

Lindsey noticing me and reporting back to Tory that they'd seen me in Enchantments? Tory was never going to believe I'd just strolled into that particular store by accident.

Or . . . would she?

"Oh my God," Lindsey cried, when I deliberately stepped out from behind the herb rack, directly into her path. "Jinx? Is that you?"

"Oh," I said, pretending to be noticing them for the first time. "Hey, you guys."

"Look, Gretch," Lindsey said. "It's Jinx!"

Gretchen, always the more serious of the pair, didn't look exactly overjoyed to see me. In fact, her heavily made-up eyes narrowed, and she said, "What are *you* doing here?" And then the gaze flicked toward something—or someone—behind me, and Gretchen's eyelids narrowed even more. "With *him*?"

"Oh, hey," Zach said, as he turned from the rack of calendars he'd been looking at.

"Hey," Lindsey said. She, unlike Gretchen, didn't seem to find it suspicious that she was running into Zach and me in a witch supply store approximately sixty blocks from where we both lived. "Is Tor here, too? I thought she said she had to go to the dentist or something this afternoon. . . ."

"Yeah," I said, nervously pushing my hair behind my ears. "Yeah, no, Tory's not here. It's just us. We came down because I have to get a gift. A birthday gift. For my little sister."

"Cool," Lindsey said. Her gaze fell on the book in my hands, and she wrinkled her nose. "But why are you getting her *that* old thing? This book's much better." She picked up the big glossy one. "Look. Lots of pictures."

"This is the one she requested," I lied. "I don't know. She's kind of weird."

"Are you saying witches are weird?" Gretchen demanded in her gravelly voice.

"No!" I cried. "Gosh, no. Just my sister."

"*I* think they're weird," Zach said cheerfully.

Lindsey reached out to give him a playful smack in the chest. "You better watch it," she said. "Or I'll put a spell on you."

"For all you know, Lindsey, maybe somebody else already has," Gretchen said. But she didn't seem to be referring to Tory, since she was looking straight at me as she said it.

"I wouldn't know anything about that," I said in as pleasant a voice as I could muster. "Well, found what I needed. Ready to go, Zach?"

"Am I ever," Zach said.

"Well, see you guys," I said to Lindsey and Gretchen. And started for the check-out counter.

"Oh, hey," Lindsey called after us. "We're gonna go get some bubble tea after this, down in Chinatown. Wanna come?"

"Can't," I said, laying the book down on the counter. The pretty saleslady picked it up with a smile. "I promised Tory's parents I'd be home in time for dinner."

"Tory," Lindsey echoed with a laugh. "Don't let her hear you call her that. She'll kill you!"

"She might kill her anyway," Gretchen muttered—but loudly enough for me to hear.

My cheeks went crimson. And the knot in my stomach swelled to a balloon.

"What?" Lindsey sounded confused. "What'd you say, Gretch?"

"Me?" Gretchen snorted. "I didn't say anything."

Zach, who had followed me, leaned down, pretending to admire some necklaces in the glass case beneath the sales counter. "What is she talking about?" he whispered.

"Nothing," I said quickly. "It's just . . . girl stuff."

"Nice," Zach said, straightening up. "How about I meet you outside?"

"That might be better," I said.

Zach nodded and left the store, the bells over the door tinkling in his wake.

"That'll be ten dollars," the woman behind the counter said. I surrendered to her my brand-new fifty.

"I bet Torrance is going to be really interested to know you were in here with her guy," Gretchen said, her voice hard.

"What?" Lindsey still sounded confused. "Gretchen? What are you talking about?"

"God, Lindsey." Gretchen flung an aggravated look in her friend's direction. "Can't you see what she's trying to do? She's trying to steal Zach right out from under Torrance's nose!"

"Zach's not Tory's guy," I burst out—as much to my own surprise as to anyone else's. The saleslady paused counting out my change, looking at me in astonishment.

"What I mean is," I said in a more modulated tone, "Zach doesn't like Tory or me. He likes Petra, okay? Zach and I are just friends."

"Right," Gretchen said, obviously not believing me. Lindsey, standing behind her, just continued to look confused.

"We're just friends," I said again, taking my change from the saleslady. I hoped Gretchen couldn't see that my hands were shaking. "You can ask him, if you want to."

"I think I'll ask Torrance," Gretchen said. "I think that's what I'll do."

"Fine," I said. "Do that."

I took the bag the saleslady was holding out for me, thanked her, and turned away from the counter and toward the door—

And knocked over a display of candles.

"God," I heard Lindsey say with a giggle, as I stooped to catch as many of the candles as I could before they rolled to the floor. "Walk much?"

"Let me, dear," the saleslady said, coming around from behind the counter.

"I'm so sorry," I said, holding an armful of candles out to her. "I'm so clumsy."

"Nonsense," the saleslady said kindly. "It could have happened to anyone. Here, put those down." She helped me put the candles down on the counter. "There. No harm done. Oh, and take this. You almost forgot it."

She took something wrapped in a neat square of tissue paper from her skirt pocket, and held it out to me.

"What . . . ?" I reached out automatically and took the paper square. Whatever was inside rattled slightly.

"Just something I think you're going to need soon," she said, her gaze sliding in Gretchen's and Lindsey's direction. "For luck. Blessings to you, sister."

My embarrassment was now consummate. I tucked the tissue-wrapped object into the bag with the book, muttered, "Thank you," and darted from the store . . .

. . . and continued down the street as if I were being chased.

"Hey," Zach called, hurrying up behind me. "Slow down, will ya? The Presidential Fitness Test is over, remember?"

"Sorry," I said, carefully not looking at him. "Oh, God. I am so embarrassed."

"Why should you be embarrassed?" He fell into step beside me.

How could he not know? Had he not—

Oh, right. He hadn't been there. Thank God. *Thank God.*

"Nothing," I said, feeling almost giddy with relief. "After you left, I . . . I walked into a display of candles and knocked them down."

"Is that all? I thought you meant the thing with Tory's

friends, thinking we're going out."

I froze in my tracks. And looked up at him. Slowly.

His green eyes were laughing down at me.

"What?" he said. "You think I don't know about Tory's little crush on me?"

The balloon in my stomach swelled to a watermelon.

"You can't say anything about it to her," I said, all in a rush. "You can't tell her that you know. And it's more than just a little crush, Zach. She seriously loves you."

"Seriously loves me, eh? That sounds like she wants to be more than just friends . . . with benefits."

He was laughing. I couldn't believe he was laughing.

"Zach," I said. "You don't understand. She isn't messing around. She—"

I almost told him. About the doll. I don't know what stopped me, exactly. Except that I felt like Tory deserved to have some dignity left to herself, in spite of her silly behavior.

"She could make life really uncomfortable for me," I said, instead, "if she thought . . . well, that you and I . . ."

Zach stopped laughing. Next thing I knew, his hands were on my shoulders.

"Hey," he said, giving me a little shake. "Cousin Jean. Cheer up. I was just kidding. The last thing in the world I want to do is make life any harder for you. I know it's tough being a preacher's kid. It must be even tougher starting a new school and living with a new family on top of your . . . well . . ."

He didn't say the word *stalker* out loud. He didn't

have to. We both knew what he was talking about, even though neither of us had ever mentioned it since that first time Tory threw it out, so casually, the day of my arrival.

"Besides," Zach said, dropping his hands away from me. "What does it matter? Considering who I'm supposed to be in love with, remember?"

Oddly enough, this reminder, instead of jabbing a stake of jealousy through my heart, did cheer me up . . . a little.

"That's right," I said. "I mean, it's totally ridiculous of those girls to think we're going out, when your heart belongs to another."

"Not just any other, either," Zach said. "But the finest piece of womanhood on the planet."

"Yeah," I said. "If they say anything about seeing us to Tory, I'll just remind her that Petra's your one true love."

"And I'll have no choice but to back you up on it," Zach said. "Eternal servitude, remember?"

Feeling a thousand times better, I turned to start back up the street, swinging my bag from Enchantments . . .

. . . and heard whatever it was the saleslady had given me rattle again. I paused, reached into the bag, and started unwrapping the tissue.

"What's that?" Zach asked.

"I don't know," I said. "Some kind of free sample or something the lady who worked there gave me . . ."

But then I saw what the tissue contained, and I

stopped in my tracks, halting so abruptly, I caused him to practically run me over .

"What?" Zach asked. "What is it?" And he looked down at what I held. "Oh, that's nice. She gave you a Satanic symbol. That's excellent customer service."

"It's not a Satanic symbol," I said in a tight voice. In the slanting rays of the setting sun, the silver necklace winked from its nest of tissue. "The pentacle is an ancient magical symbol, meant to offer spiritual protection for its wearer. It has nothing to do with Satan."

Zach said in a gentle voice, "Hey, Jean. I was kidding again, all right?"

Horrified to find my eyes welling up with tears right there on the sidewalk outside a small body-piercing boutique, I slipped the necklace back into the bag, then hugged the bag to my chest.

For luck, she had said. *Just something I think you're going to need soon.*

How had she known?

A better question, though, was *what* did she know that I didn't?

CHAPTER NINE

"What are you doing in my room?"

Tory's voice was laced with venom. She'd flicked on the overhead light, and now she stood in the doorway, her leather jacket shrugged half-off, staring at me.

Coming awake slowly, I lifted my head from where it had sunk onto one of Tory's pillows, and blinked in the sudden flood of light. I must, I realized, have fallen asleep waiting for Tory to come home. The book I'd purchased earlier that evening lay across my chest, open, I knew, to the chapter on banishing spells.

"Tory," I said groggily, sitting up. "Where have you been? What time is it?"

"What does it matter what time it is?" Tory snapped. "What are you doing in my room? That's the real question."

I shoved some hair out of my eyes and squinted at the digital alarm clock on Tory's nightstand. "Jeez," I said.

"It's almost midnight. Your parents are going to be mad—"

"They're not even home yet themselves," Tory said. She flung off her leather jacket, letting it fall to the floor, where most of the rest of her clothes would lay until Marta came in to clean. "What are you doing in here, anyway? And why aren't you with *Zach*?"

So they'd told her. That hadn't taken long.

"Tory," I said, swinging my legs over the side of the bed. I'd grown so tired waiting for Tory, I'd changed into my pajamas. Now my bare feet sank into the deep lavender pile that carpeted her room as I stood up. "Nothing's going on between Zach and me. We're just friends. You know as well as I do that he's in love with Petra. We need to talk about something else. It's important."

Tory had gone into her walk-in closet the minute I'd mentioned Petra, having lost interest in the conversation. She must have known, the whole time Gretchen or whoever was telling her about seeing Zach and me together, that it couldn't be true about the two of us.

Because now, having emerged from her closet wearing only a black bra, her miniskirt, and a lot of necklaces, her heavily—but expertly—made-up eyes went wide. That's because she'd finally noticed the book.

"So that's why you went to Enchantments," she said. "I knew it wasn't to get a birthday present for Courtney. Courtney's birthday's not till February. Did you change your mind?" she asked eagerly. "You thought about what I said, about joining our coven?"

I shook my head. This, I knew, was going to take some guts. But I had no choice. I really didn't.

No matter how much my stomach hurt.

"No," I said. "I want to talk to you about this."

From inside the front cover of the book I was still holding, I pulled Petra's photograph, the one from the litter box, and held it out for Tory to see. It was in a sealed Ziploc bag, but you could still see what it was.

Tory squinted at it, then made a face.

"Ew," she said. "You TOUCHED it? That isn't very hygienic, you know. I hope you washed your hands."

Then, when I didn't say anything more, she shrugged. "So. You found it. I wondered if you would. Well. You want to know why it was in there?"

"I know why it was in there," I said. "What I want to know is why you did it."

Tory just shrugged again, then sat down on the tasseled swivel stool in front of her dressing table, where she began brushing her thick black hair.

"Why do I have to explain myself to you?" she asked my reflection.

"Because this is serious." I crossed the room to stand beside the dressing table, and looked down at her. "Maybe you didn't know, but what you did—taping Petra's picture to the bottom of Mouche's box like that—it's black magic, Tory. It's bad."

Tory stared at my refection incredulously for a beat. Then she let out a whoop of laughter.

"Listen to you!" she cried. "Black magic! You kill me!"

"I'm serious, Tory," I said. I held up the book I'd bought. "It says so right here. Magic spells used to bring harm to another are really dangerous. It inevitably comes back to the person who cast it, like a boomerang. But times three."

"Well, look at you." Tory grinned up at me, her smile distinctly feline. "And I thought you didn't believe."

"Seriously, Tory," I said. "I'm worried about you. Why would you do something like that, and to Petra, of all people? Petra is one of the sweetest, kindest people I've ever met. She's never done anything to you. So what have you got against her? Is it just because Zach likes her? Is that it? Because what you're doing . . . it's wrong. It's mean-spirited and wrong. I don't know why you did this to her, but I'm telling you right now, it's over."

"Oh," Tory said, not smiling now. "It's over. Right."

"I mean it, Tory. You and this coven of yours can play around at being witches all you want. You can make up little spells and perform them on each other and have a grand old time, for all I care. But not spells that manipulate or hurt other people. Especially people like Petra."

"Oh, yeah?" Tory tossed her head. "And exactly how are you going to stop me?"

"Well." I looked down at the floor. I had expected this to go so differently. I don't know why. I mean, knowing Tory, I shouldn't have expected her to be anything but mad.

But in my head, when I'd rehearsed this conversation, Tory had apologized and said she hadn't known what she'd been doing to Petra was so harmful. She'd thanked me for telling her, and we'd hugged and gone downstairs for cocoa together.

It didn't look like it was going to go that way after all. I was glad I'd made backup preparations, just in case. I sighed.

"The truth is, Tor," I said, raising my gaze to meet hers, "I've bound you."

"You've bound—" Tory gaped at me. "You've *what*?"

"Bound you from performing evil." I stood my ground. "You can still work positive spells. But not ones that manipulate anyone's will. They won't work. Not anymore."

Tory looked as shocked as if I had slapped her. "You hypocritical little . . . are you telling me that this whole time—all this time—you really *have* been one of us?"

"I'm *not* one of you," I said firmly. "I'll admit I might have been interested in magic once. But it . . . it didn't work out. Okay, Tory? It went really, really wrong, and someone got hurt, and I swore to myself I never would do it again. Magic, I mean. It's serious business, Tory, and not something anyone who doesn't know what they're doing should mess around with."

Tory made a face. "Thanks for the tip, *Mom*. But it might interest you to know I *do* know what I'm doing."

"No, you don't. Not if *this* is an example." I held up Petra's battered photo. "Something like this could really hurt someone. That's why—even though I didn't want to—I had to break my promise to myself never to do magic again, and bind you."

"Oh," Tory said, slapping both hands to her face in mock horror. "Oh, don't, Cousin Jinx! I'm so scared. I'm sure your stupid *hick* magic is so much more powerful than mine." She dropped her hands and eyed me with total contempt. "Let's get one thing straight, *Sabrina*. This is New York City, not Iowa. I suspect my magic's just a teensy bit more sophisticated than yours. So whatever crappy little binding spell you've done on me, you better not count on it working. Because here in the big city, Jinx, we don't mess around."

"We don't mess around in Iowa, either," I pointed out quietly. "In fact, my spells have always worked just fine." Actually, I'd only done one. But still. It HAD worked. Unfortunately, a little *too* well.

"Oh, right!" Tory threw back her head and laughed. "You're clearly such a powerful witch! Let me see . . . you and your white-trash parents live in a house that's too small for you, with, like, one bathroom. You're not allowed to listen to rap or watch HBO. You're a straight-A, knock-kneed orchestra geek. And you had to move to New York to live off the charity of your rich relatives, because some boy in your town got a crush on you, and your parents freaked."

She'd stood up now and was facing me with her hands on her hips, a scornful expression on her face, her nose just inches from mine.

"Oh, yeah," she went on sarcastically. "You're a huge powerful witch, all right. I'm so scared. Because you've obviously cast so many spells that worked. NOT."

I thought about hitting her. I really did. Not so much because of the geek thing—let's face it: I *am* an orchestra geek (I'm not knock-kneed, though). But because of the thing about my family being white trash. I mean, my parents totally make enough money to get by. Okay, maybe we don't get Rolexes for Christmas like the kids around here do.

But my parents have never taken clothes for us from the church donation box. It's true Courtney's sick of getting all of my hand-me-downs. But not everyone can afford to buy their kids an all-new wardrobe every year. . . .

But I didn't. Hit her, I mean. I've never hit anybody in my life, and I wasn't about to start with Tory, however sorely she might tempt me.

I wanted to hurt her, though. Seriously hurt her.

Which was horrible, because I could tell she was *already* hurting. On the inside, from completely self-inflicted wounds. I had no idea why Tory was so insecure, but that had to have been why she'd lashed out at me like that . . . why she would do—or try to do, anyway—what she had to Petra.

This witch thing—this story she'd heard about our ancestress, Branwen—it had gone to her head. She was clinging to it, like a life raft, because she felt as if she had nothing else to hold on to. She didn't like herself enough to . . . well, just *be* herself.

The thing was . . . I knew the feeling.

I also knew, only too well, where it could lead.

But what I couldn't understand was how she'd gotten this way.

"What *happened* to you, Tory?" I asked her. "You weren't like this five years ago. What happened to make you so . . . mean?"

Tory narrowed her eyes at me. "Five years ago? You mean when I was the most unpopular girl in school, because I was a fat, boring doormat who let the other girls walk all over me and the only thing boys wanted from me was help with their homework? I'll tell you what happened, Jinx. Grandma told me about Branwen. And I realized that the blood of a sorceress runs through my veins. I realized that I had power . . . real power, to make people do what I wanted them to do . . . or crush them if they didn't. I just had to take control. Of my life. Of my destiny."

"Oh," I said sarcastically. "Is that what you're doing in the boiler room with Shawn during your free period every day? Taking control of your destiny?"

Tory looked at me coldly. "God," she said. "You're such a child. I should have known you wouldn't understand."

It was pointless. I realized that now. I took my book and Petra's photo, and turned to go.

At the doorway, however, I hesitated, and gave it one last try. "About Zach . . ."

Tory glared at me. "What about him?"

I knew I should have just dropped it. It wasn't worth it. And it wasn't going to make any difference.

Still, that thing she'd said about my parents . . . it had gotten to me. A little.

"Just don't stick any more pins in that doll's head," I said.

Tory cocked a hip. "And what if I do?"

"You'll just be wasting your time."

"Oh, yeah?" Tory's voice was no longer derisive. Now it was filled with hatred. Pure and simple. "Well, we'll see about that, won't we? We'll see how big a waste of time you think it is, when Zach ends up with me—not Petra, and certainly not *you*. Because you know what? No matter how much you two hang around together, talking about freaking *Seventh Heaven*, or whatever, he's going to be mine. I've willed it. *I'm* the one with the gift, Jinx. You may have gotten the red hair, but I got the magic. I realize that now. Branwen meant Grandma's grand-daughter, not granddaughter*s*, would have the gift. And that granddaughter is me. Because I'm not afraid to use her gift, the way you are. What do you think of that?"

I thought fleetingly of the woman behind the counter at the witch store, of her gentle greeting—"Blessed be!"—and the kindness with which she insisted I take the pentacle necklace, which I now wore. So different, so starkly different, from the kind of witch Tory thought she was. Or wanted to be.

"I don't know that I'd go around bragging about what you think you've inherited from our great-great-great-great-grandmother, if I were you, Tory," I said.

"Why not?"

"Didn't Grandma mention how she died?" I asked.

Tory shook her head, looking curious, in spite of herself.

"She was burned to death at the stake," I said. "For practicing witchcraft."

Then I left her room, closing the door behind me.

CHAPTER TEN

"I cannot believe it." Petra's hand was shaking as she dropped a stack of pancakes onto my plate. "I still cannot believe it. In a week he will be here. Just one week! It is too good to be true."

Carefully avoiding Tory's sullen gaze, I picked up the syrup pitcher and said, "Well, I think it's great, Petra. I can't wait to meet him."

"Willem," Teddy said, shoveling a forkful of pancake into his mouth, "is cool. How long's he staying, Petra?"

"Ten days." Petra's blue eyes had not stopped dancing since she'd put down the phone. "Ten days, all travel expenses paid! Do you know how much a ticket from my country to New York costs?"

Alice said, "Maybe I should start listening to the radio. Maybe I could win a new bike. I really need a new bike."

Petra, despite her euphoria, was still Petra, and she

said with gentle asperity, "Alice, you have a lovely bicycle that you got only last Christmas."

"Yes," Alice said. "But it's a baby's bike, with pedal brakes. I want a grown-up bike, like Teddy's, with handle-bar brakes. Maybe I could win one over the radio, like Willem won a trip to New York."

Tory glared sourly at her little sister over the cup of coffee she'd poured herself. "Just ask Dad, for God's sake," she said. "He'll buy you a damned bike."

Petra flicked Tory a glance, since both Teddy and Alice began chortling at the mention of the D word, but she didn't say anything. I hastened to change the subject.

"If you want to take a day off to spend with Willem, and you need someone to watch these two," I said, giving my giggling little cousins a mock stern look, "just let me know."

Petra gave me a glorious smile. "Thank you, Jean. I will."

Tory made a face and mouthed, *Brown nose*, at me.

I ignored her.

Then later, as we were leaving the house for school, Tory snapped, "Don't think, Jinx, that Petra's boyfriend winning this stupid trip has anything to do with your taking that photo out of Mouche's box. Or with your dumb binding spell."

I kept my face carefully blank. "I wouldn't dream of thinking any such thing," I said.

"Because I did a little binding spell of my own last

night," Tory said. "We'll see how well your little country-bumpkin magic works against the real thing."

"I guess we will," I said, wondering how it had gotten to this: my cousin and me, fighting over who was the more powerful witch. I mean, talk about stupid.

I couldn't help feeling a little guilty. In a way, Tory had a right to be angry: to her, I probably did seem like the world's biggest hypocrite, pretending not to know what she was talking about, that first night I'd arrived. When I *had* known. I'd known perfectly well. Grandma had told me the same story—about how into my generation would be born the next great witch in the family. It had just been a bedtime story, told to entertain.

But it had made quite an impression on me when I'd heard it—the same impression it had obviously made on Tory. Because, like Tory, I'd been convinced I knew who the witch of my generation was:

Me. Of course it was me. My name was Jinx, wasn't it? That, coupled with the red hair and the story surrounding my birth . . . I had to be the witch. *I* was the freak. *I* was the unlucky one.

To everyone else in my family, though, it was just a story Grandma told, to get us interested in our family tree. She clearly didn't believe it herself. She always laughed as she told it, like it was the most hilarious thing ever.

But she didn't laugh when, the last time she came to visit us, I told her that I had found out what happened to Branwen, her great-great-grandmother. Grandma had conveniently left off the part about Branwen being the last woman to be burned to death for witchcraft in Wales, the country she was from—a fact easily confirmed on the Internet.

I had looked up the name on a lark, bored in computer lab one day. I'd stared at the screen, feeling my blood run cold. Because suddenly, it wasn't just a story. It really *was* true. I *was* the descendant of a witch.

Grandma had been philosophical about it.

"Oh, well," she said. "I'm sure Branwen was a good witch. She was a healer, you know. She probably did a better job of curing people than the town alchemist, so he got jealous and accused her of witchcraft. You know how things were back then." Grandma had just finished *The Da Vinci Code*. "It was all politics."

Politics or not, a relative of mine had been killed—killed!—for witchcraft. It was clearly nothing to mess around with.

Something I'd learned the hard way when, despite what I knew about Branwen, I'd cast my first spell and watched it go so tragically wrong.

Which was why I knew Tory—whether or not she had "the gift" Grandma promised one (or both) of us had inherited from Branwen—had to be stopped.

So while Petra had been putting Teddy and Alice to bed the night before, I had snuck down into her basement apartment, and furtively placed a penny, heads up, in each corner of Petra's bedroom. Then I'd sprinkled some sea salt over the threshold of every door leading to and from Petra's apartment.

Finally, I'd written Tory's name down on a sheet of white paper, and buried it beneath the ice cube trays in Petra's refrigerator. Petra would puzzle over this, surely, if she ever found it, but at least she'd be safe. . . .

But it was going to be hard, I could tell, to convince Tory that what she was doing was wrong. It was Grandma's fault, really, for filling her head—not to mention mine—with all that talk about our destinies. If I had never heard I was descended from a witch, I might never have picked up that first book on witchcraft, the one I'd found in my school library back in Hancock, the one I'd used to cast that first spell, the one that had so completely changed my life . . .

. . . and, unfortunately, someone else's, as well.

But if I'd never cast that first spell, then, of course, I never would have come to New York.

And I never would have met Zach.

Really, when I thought about it, all of it—the thing back home, and the pain and loneliness of being away from my family and starting over at a new school—seemed worth it, when I took into account that it had enabled me to meet Zach.

Zach, who, it was true, was in love with someone else. But who also, without prompting from any magic, white or black, was still my friend.

And that was something. That was *really* something.

Still, taking everything that had happened between us into account, I wasn't particularly surprised when

Tory started giving me the cold shoulder. I'd actually been wondering why it hadn't happened before now. The only rational explanation was that Tory liked having someone around she could pick on mercilessly. And since I try not to take Tory's snide remarks to heart, I hadn't really minded being that person.

But when I approached Tory's lunch table the morning Petra announced Willem's contest win, she looked up at me and said, "Don't . . . even . . . think . . . about . . . it."

Well. Even a country girl like me can take a hint.

I took my tray and went to sit at the table where I'd frequently seen my fellow orchestra members sitting. There were none there yet, but I hoped that, when they did show up, they wouldn't choose to sit somewhere else when they saw me there. In order not to look so conspicuously friendless, I pulled my U.S. History textbook from my bag and flipped it open.

I had barely made it through a page on Alexander Hamilton when another tray slammed down next to mine. I looked up and saw Chanelle slide into the chair beside mine.

"God," Chanelle said, prying open a can of diet soda. "Your cousin is *such* a *bitch*."

I raised my eyebrows. It apparently wasn't necessary for me to reply, since Chanelle went right on talking.

"Like, I can put up with the partying. I love a good party myself. But not *every night*." Chanelle widened her brown eyes meaningfully. "A girl's got to get her beauty sleep. I can't be out past midnight every night. First of all, my dermatologist would kill me, but secondly, bags." She pointed at her eyelids. "See them? They're there. Bags. *Bags*. And I'm only sixteen years old.

"But that's not the only thing." Chanelle gnawed on a carrot stick. "It's these new friends of hers. Those so-called witches, Gretchen and Lindsey? Look, I am totally open to new things. I even went to one of their meetings. You know, a witch meeting. It was so bogus. All these girls in black running around, summoning the spirit of the East . . . I was like, Uh, could someone please tell me what happened on *Grey's Anatomy* last night?" Chanelle's voice dipped dramatically. "*But nobody there knew*. Now what is up with that?"

I sipped my own soda and then said, "Maybe it's just a phase. Maybe she'll get tired of it soon."

"Not her." Chanelle started to unwrap a Hostess cupcake. Chanelle's theory, apparently, was that if she ate nothing else for lunch but diet soda and carrot sticks, she could reward herself with dessert. "Ever since she heard about that great-great-great-grandma of hers, she changed. It's like she turned into Paris Hilton, or somebody. Only without the fun shopping and the Chihuahua. Suddenly it's all about parties and black nail polish and putting curses on people. I'm telling you, she really thinks she's a witch. And it was all right—I totally respect other people's religions, and all that—but then she started threatening to put spells on people. First it was just teachers and boys and the bitchy senior girls, you know? But then it was *me*. I can take quite a lot, but being told that someone's put a spell on me because I won't help her dig for mushrooms in the waxing light of the moon . . ."

"Dig for *what* in the waxing light of the moon?" I asked.

"I don't know. Some mushrooms that only grow on headstones. She asked me just now to come with her to some cemetery down on Wall Street in the middle of the night and help her scrape mushrooms off some crumbling old tombstones. . . . Well, I told her to forget it. I'm not hanging around any old cemetery, and besides, Robert and I have plans tonight, you know? He *is* my boyfriend, after all, even though he's kind of lame. Still, he's cute when he's not high. I just wish he would stop hanging around that stupid Shawn guy. I don't know what Torrance sees in him. I really don't. That boy is bad news. But he's popular. So Tor meets him in the boiler room every day. . . ." She shook her head until the springy braids her hair was done up in bounced.

"Anyway, you know what she told me? She told me she didn't need my help, since her REAL friends would help her. Meaning Gretchen and Lindsey, of course. So I said, 'Fine, if your REAL friends are so great, you can just eat lunch with them.' And she went, 'Fine, at least my REAL friends have something to talk about besides shopping.' And I went . . ."

Mushrooms off a tombstone? What, I wondered, could Tory be up to?

"Look," Chanelle said eventually, scooping a fingerful of filling from her cupcake, "I like you, Jinx. You're kind of a geek, with that violin of yours, and all, but you don't put people down, and it seems like you aren't all hung up on witchcraft or clothes or your weight or getting into the right college, like everybody else around here. You wanna be my new best friend?"

I'd been taking a sip of soda as Chanelle asked this—which was why I nearly choked. It was so like Chanelle—what I knew of her, anyway—simply to come out and ask something like that. *Wanna be my new best friend?* How on earth could I possibly say no to a request like that, even if I'd wanted to?

Which, I found, I didn't. I liked Chanelle.

And I figured Stacy, with whom I still IMed nightly, would understand.

"Sure," I said. "But, um, just until you make up with Tory. Because I know Tory really loves you, Chanelle. She's just going through a tough time right now. In fact, maybe what we should do is let her know that we're here for her, whenever she's ready to, um, calm down."

"Or," Chanelle said, "not. I'm tired of her bossing me around. Hey, wanna come over after school today? I'm trying to decide on a hairstyle for the spring formal. Robert's taking me. We could give each other makeovers. I would LOVE to get my hands on that hair of yours. Have you ever considered wearing it up?"

I said, "No. But, sure, I'd love to." No one had ever invited me over to her house to try out hairstyles.

Chanelle said, *"Excellent!"* Then she sobered. "But I think I better warn you: I'm not the only one Tory's putting a spell on. She says she's putting one on you, too."

I took a bite of my salad. "Really?" I kept my voice carefully devoid of emotion.

"Yeah. She's real upset about you and Zach." Chanelle looked a little like a bird as she cocked her head at me and asked, "Are you two going out, or something?"

I couldn't help smiling. Any mention of Zach's name seemed to have that effect on me. It was pathetic.

"No," I said. "We're just friends."

"Well, you guys spend enough time together. My friend Camille says you two skip P.E. together every day."

"He's in love with our au pair," I said hastily. "Honest."

"Yeah, well, that's not what Tory thinks. She thinks you're purposefully trying to steal Zach from her. She says she's gonna put such a spell on you, you're gonna wish you never came here from Idaho."

"Iowa," I said.

"Whatever." Chanelle shuddered, even though we were sitting in a puddle of bright sunlight, slanting through the cafeteria windows. "I don't know, Jinx. I don't believe in that witchcraft stuff, but the way she said it . . . it scared me. I'd watch out if I were you. Like, it's all right for me. I don't have to live in the same house as her. But you'd better watch your back."

"Thanks for the warning, but I can handle it. I think

all of Tory's spells are over. In fact," I added, as I watched Tory throw what was left of her lunch away and, casting a scathing look in our direction, leave the cafeteria, "I can pretty much guarantee it."

CHAPTER ELEVEN

It actually seemed that way—at least that day. That Tory's spell-casting days were over.

That evening, when I returned from Chanelle's house, Petra was bubbling over with yet more good news.

"I got the only A in my entire Glyconutrition class," she gushed, the minute I walked into the kitchen in search of a soda.

"Wow," I said. "Congratulations, Petra."

"So many good things in one day," Petra said, with a happy sigh. "I cannot believe it!"

"I can't believe it, either," I said.

"Oh, and Jean. Zach called, from next door. Here is the message. He asks that you call him back."

I didn't bother going to my own room to return Zach's call. It didn't even occur to me. Instead, I took the slip of paper Petra handed me and dialed it on the kitchen telephone, wondering what Zach could have to say, since I'd already spent an hour with him that afternoon, feeding bits of pretzel to some ducks in Central Park, having slipped away from the softball game Coach Winthrop had organized for our class at the baseball diamond. Zach had taken the bad news—about Willem's impending visit to Manhattan—quite manfully, in my opinion.

"Oh, good, it's you." The sound of Zach's deep voice sent ripples of pleasure up the back of my arms. "Guess what?"

"What?"

"Well, you know how my dad gets free tickets to stuff all the time, through work, right?"

"Yeah," I said.

"Well, someone gave him two tickets for Saturday night to see this violinist at Carnegie Hall. He doesn't want to go, but I know how much you like the violin, so I thought maybe you'd heard of this guy—Nigel Kennedy—" I couldn't restrain a gasp. Zach, sounding like he was laughing, went on. "Yeah. That's what I thought. He's supposed to be good. So I wondered if you'd be interested. I thought I'd come along—as a friend, of course. I mean, unless you'd rather take someone from orchestra, or something."

Nigel Kennedy! I couldn't believe it!

"Oh, my gosh, Zach," I screeched into the phone. "That sounds great! But are you sure you won't be bored?"

"I think I can probably handle it," Zach said. "You can always prod me if I fall asleep."

I sucked in my breath happily—then held it, as Tory strode into the kitchen from the garden outside and stood glaring darkly at me from the doorway.

Had she overheard?

"I thought maybe we could have dinner or something, beforehand," Zach went on. "As friends, of course. Maybe you could give me some more tips about how I could win over Petra."

"Ha," I said into the phone. She'd overheard, all right. Her glare was growing more menacing by the second. "Okay. That sounds great."

"Cool," he said. "See you at school."

"See you then." I hung up. Tory, still leaning in the doorway, eyed me.

"So," she said. "You and Zach are going out tonight?"

"Saturday night," I said. "And just as friends. It's not a date or anything. His dad got a couple of free tickets to see Nigel Kennedy, the British violinist, at Carnegie Hall, and Zach wanted to know if I was interested in going with him. . . ."

Tory eyed me expressionlessly. "I didn't know Zach liked classical music."

"Well . . ." I glanced at Petra, who was standing a few feet away, chopping vegetables. Other than the fact that her shoulders had gotten kind of tense, Petra gave no sign she was paying attention to our conversation. "I don't know. Maybe he wants to expand his horizons or something."

"Isn't that sweet," Tory said in a tone that implied she

thought it was anything but. "What happened to your hair?"

I reached up instinctively to touch my hair. I'd forgotten that Chanelle had been experimenting on it earlier in the evening. She'd brushed it into a crazy bouffant that she'd then insisted I wear home.

"Oh," I said. "That was Chanelle. We were just messing around over at her house."

"Well," Tory said. "How nice. First you steal my boyfriend. Then you steal my best friend. Is that how they do things back in Iowa? Because it sure isn't how we do things here."

Trying to keep my temper, I said, "You know perfectly well Zach doesn't like me as anything except a friend. And he was never your boyfriend. You *have* a boyfriend. Shawn, remember?" I didn't want to bring up the "friends with benefits" thing in front of Petra, so I just added, "And Chanelle feels like, ever since you started hanging out with Gretchen and Lindsey, you don't care about her anymore. You don't seem to want to spend time with her. So why shouldn't I?"

"I don't care who you spend time with," Tory said scornfully. "I'm just wondering why you have to spend so *much* time with this guy you claim isn't even interested in you. Like it isn't enough for you that you get to spend fifth period with him every single day. Oh, no. Now you have to go to a *concert* with him, too."

I glanced at Petra. She was still chopping away.

"Look, Tory," I said. "If it's going to make you upset,

I'll just call him and tell him I can't make it—"

Because what else could I say?

But Tory didn't seem to like that idea, either.

"Oh, no," she said. "Don't not go on *my* account. *I* don't care how you waste your time. It's yours to waste. By all means, go see a classical concert with Zach Rosen. What do *I* care? When it's through, maybe the two of you can stroll on over to Central Park, since you seem to like it so much. Wouldn't *that* be fun? Good, clean fun. Because God knows Cousin Jean from Iowa would never do anything *bad*. Except skip P.E., of course."

I glanced at Petra, who'd given up pretending not to be eavesdropping. She'd turned from the cutting board and was totally listening, her gaze focused on Tory, her expression inscrutable.

"I wonder what Coach Winthrop would say if he found out what you two were up to," Tory said musingly. "You and Zach. Every fifth period. You know, Coach Winthrop can't stand it when people skip his class. . . ."

I swallowed. "Is that supposed to be some kind of threat, Tory?" I asked.

Tory laughed. She'd changed out of her school uniform into another of her black minidresses. This one appeared to be made out of leather.

"No," she said. "This is: I wonder how *friendly* Zach would feel toward you if I happened to mention to him that that book you bought at Enchantments wasn't for your sister, after all, but for your own personal use—"

"Torrance," Petra said.

Tory had been walking slowly toward me as she spoke. Now she whirled around impatiently. "What?" she practically yelled at Petra.

Petra, however, was perfectly calm as she said, "Your mother called me from her office today. She says your guidance counselor contacted her at work. Your mother wants me to make sure you're home for dinner tonight, so she and your father can talk to you. I think you know what it is about. So please stay home tonight, all right?"

Tory didn't say anything right away. Instead, she flashed a look of pure hatred in my direction. The look said all too clearly, *You did this, didn't you?*

I shook my head. Of course I hadn't! Whatever this was, Tory had brought it all upon herself.

But it was too late. Much too late.

Tory let out a laugh that didn't have any humor in it.

"That's it," she said. "This is war, Jinx."

Then she turned around and ran from the kitchen. A few seconds later, we heard the front door slam, hard enough to cause the windows to rattle.

Petra was the one who broke the silence that followed.

"You listen to me, Jinx," she said. "You go to that thing, that violin thing. Go with Zach."

I shook my head. "No, Petra. It's not worth it. Not if it's going to upset her so much. It's all right, really."

Because what was the point? Tory was just going to tell Zach, at her earliest opportunity, about my spell-casting past . . . what she knew of it, anyway, which thankfully wasn't much. And he'd realize I'm as big a freak—if not an even bigger one—than her, and drop me like a hot potato.

"No, it's *not* all right," Petra said, raising her voice for the first time since I'd met her—to me, anyway. Startled, I stared at her. "There is something wrong in this house. I know this. And I am telling you, what is wrong in this house is *that one*." Petra pointed with her paring knife in the direction Tory had just gone. "It is not fair of her to tell you this, that you cannot see Zachary. He does not belong to her. He has never made her any promise. You go with him."

"It's not worth it, Petra," I said. "It'll just make her angry."

"She is already angry." Petra turned back to her carrots. "You let *me* deal with her anger. I am used to it."

I couldn't help smiling a little at Petra's strong, slender back. She had no idea what she was talking about. It really *was* funny, if you thought about it.

"And what did she mean by that?" the au pair whipped around to demand. "What did she mean about a war?"

"Nothing," I said. I reached up and touched the pentacle that hung around my neck.

It looked like I was going to be needing the good luck it was supposed to bring me a little sooner than I'd expected.

CHAPTER TWELVE

It started the next day.

I knew it as I approached my locker, before first period had even begun. I stopped suddenly, the traffic in the hallway streaming around me, people giving me annoyed looks as they tried to get by.

There'd been no sign of Tory that morning, and, having noticed the tenseness in Aunt Evelyn's face at the breakfast table (apparently the little meeting she and Uncle Ted had had with Tory the night before, when Tory had finally turned up again, had not gone well), I hadn't waited for her, and had just gone on to school without her.

Zach—whom I'd run into on my way to school—looked around the hallway and went, "What is it?"

"Look," I said. And pointed.

The halls of the Chapman School are usually crowded. The exclusive school, whose graduates routinely go on to Ivy League colleges, was experiencing a surge of popularity that had resulted in classrooms that were almost spilling over, and hallways that were barely passable. But that day they seemed even more so.

Then I realized that the crowd was not made up of the kids I normally saw lingering outside their classrooms waiting for the bell to ring, but teachers and even some administrators from the principal's office, too. They were all standing around, staring at one spot . . . and that spot, I knew, even from a hundred feet away, was my locker.

With a growing feeling of dread—not to mention the resurrection of the knot in my stomach—I pushed my way past a couple of lacrosse players who were blocking my view, then stumbled to a halt. There, hanging by a shoelace from the vent in the top half of my locker door, was a dead rat. Fluid of some kind—not blood—dripped from the cavity where the rat's head should have been, forming a pinkish puddle on the tile floor in front of my locker.

Zach squeezed through the crowd behind me, and then froze. I felt his breath, warm on the back of my neck, as he whispered, "Holy—"

A maintenance worker was carefully unstringing the rat, a plastic bag held open beneath it to receive the body as it fell. It did, with a sickeningly soft thud. Several students groaned.

"Is this your locker, young lady?" a sharp-nosed administrator asked me.

I could not take my gaze off the pink puddle in front of my locker door.

"Yes, ma'am," I said.

"Do you have any idea who could have done this?"

I lifted my gaze from the puddle, but instead of fastening it on the administrator's face, I scanned the crowd, searching it for one person in particular. I finally noticed Tory pressed up against the shoulders of the lacrosse players, peering around them, a triumphant smile plastered on her face.

I looked away and said to the administrator, "No, ma'am. I have no idea who could have done this."

I went through the rest of the day in a sort of haze. What, I kept asking myself, did Tory think she was doing? Stealing a dissection rat from the bio lab—because that, I learned, is where the rat had come from. The fluid dripping from its open neck had been formaldehyde—cutting off its head, and hanging it upside down outside someone's locker wasn't witchcraft, black or white. It wasn't *magic* at all. It was just sick. Was this how Tory intended to punish me for binding her from doing magic? By showing me how powerful she could be without using magic at all?

Well, it was working. I was scared—not of the rat, but of what it represented. If someone could do that to a rat—even an already dead one—who knew what they'd do to a cat . . . or an innocent au pair.

How could my protection spells—putting pennies in the four corners of a room, or writing someone's name on a piece of paper and putting it in a freezer—keep someone safe from the kind of dangerous pranks Tory and her friends liked to perform?

Because that's all they were. Pranks . . . foolish pranks. Certainly not magic, and certainly not funny. They were enough, in fact, to make the most even-tempered of people angry.

"There's no way we can prove it was her," Chanelle said at lunch that day, glaring at the table where Tory and Gretchen and Lindsey normally sat . . . which was conspicuously empty today. They seemed to have chosen to eat elsewhere. "They'll never expel her without proof. She'll just figure out who told, and then she'll do something even worse to that person. She and those witchy friends of hers."

"They *aren't* witches," I said adamantly. "They're playing at being witches. The ability to make magic—real magic—is a gift, a life-affirming gift. People who have that gift follow a moral code, a code which seeks to build harmony with nature and among people, not harm them."

Even Robert, chowing down on a bacon cheeseburger, looked impressed by my speech. "Wow," he said. "Where'd you hear that? The Discovery Channel?"

I said, "No. I . . . I read it somewhere."

"Then what about the rat?" Chanelle demanded. "That wasn't very life-affirming."

"That's exactly what I'm trying to say," I said. "That wasn't witchcraft."

"It was just plain deluded," Chanelle said. She looked at Shawn, who was busy typing into his Treo. "Dude. She's your girlfriend. Can't you say something to her? Like if she doesn't calm down, you're not going to take her to the spring formal after all?"

"She's not my girlfriend," Shawn said, not even looking up from the screen. "I told you. And I have to take her. I already bought the tickets and put a down payment on the limo."

"Take someone else," Chanelle said.

That did make Shawn look up from the screen.

"If I tell her I'm taking someone else," Shawn said, wide-eyed, "she'll hang a rat from *my* locker. Or worse."

"Are you saying you're afraid of your own girlfriend?" Chanelle demanded.

"Hell, yeah," Shawn said. "Besides, what do I wanna make her mad for? She provides a valuable service for me every day during free period."

"You're disgusting," Chanelle declared. Then, looking sadly at me, she said, "Sorry, Jean. I guess there's still nothing we can do about it."

Nothing we can do about it. The phrase echoed through my head for the rest of the afternoon. It couldn't be true. There had to be *something* we could do—something *I* could do. Only *what*?

"I know it was Tory," Zach informed me matter-of-factly, when fifth period rolled around. "And it's time someone did something about her."

"Please don't get involved," I said. Clouds had finally moved over Manhattan, and instead of conducting his P.E. classes in the streaming rain, Coach Winthrop was forcing his students to play dodgeball in the cafeteria. I had promptly allowed myself to be struck by the ball, and a minute later, Zach joined me, sitting with our backs against the wall, along with the other people who'd been struck out.

"I'm already involved," Zach said. "Come on, Jean, I'm not stupid. I don't know what's going on between you two, but I have my suspicions, and I'm not going to let her—"

"I mean it, Zach," I said. I concentrated on relacing my running shoes, so he wouldn't see how close I was to crying. "Just stay out of it, okay?"

He didn't look the least bit cowed. "Why? Why do I have to stay out of it? I'm the one who's causing it, aren't I?"

"Not exactly," I said. I knew what I had to do—where Zach was concerned, anyway. I just really, really didn't want to do it.

But what choice did I have? Either I told him the truth . . . or Tory would tell him her version of it. At least if I did it, there was a chance—a small one, I'll admit— that he might understand.

Because there was so much more to the story than Tory knew.

"There's a little more to it," I began awkwardly, wondering how on earth I could ever make him understand, "than just Tory's crush on you."

But to my surprise, he made things much, much easier by reaching out and touching the pentacle hanging around my neck.

"Is it this stuff?" he wanted to know. "Witch stuff?"

Something caught in my throat. I think it was the knot from my stomach.

"Yeah," I said, after coughing. "That day we went to Enchantments, down in the Village . . . I didn't . . . I didn't quite tell you the truth—"

"You mean that that book you bought was for you, and not Courtney?" The look he threw me was on the sarcastic side. "I may not have ESP like you do, Jean. But I did manage to figure out that part for myself."

"I . . . I don't have ESP," I stammered.

"Right. How did you know that bike messenger was going to ram into me? How'd you know the exact moment to shove me out of the way?"

"That was just . . . that was just . . ." My voice trailed off. His green-eyed gaze held me hypnotized.

"Jean, I know you have . . . well, special talents," he said. "But you don't actually believe all that witch stuff really works, do you? The magic and spells and voodoo mumbo-jumbo? You don't, do you?"

Tearing my gaze from his with an effort, and keeping it, instead, on the dodgeball game, I said, "I . . . do, Zach. The thing is, I've seen things . . . things that couldn't be explained any other way than by magic."

137

"Ancient civilizations used the concept of magic to explain anything they couldn't understand . . . like illness," Zach said grimly. "But we know better now, because of science. Just because there's no other explanation that we happen to know of, doesn't mean it's magic."

"I know," I said. "But that doesn't negate the fact that . . . I believe. And what's more important, Tory does, too."

"Well, it's got to stop. It's not right. Whatever it is Tory's doing . . . I'm not just going to stand by and watch like everyone else in this school does. I'm not going to let her get away with it."

I hung my head. "Don't. Seriously, Zach, don't. Tory . . . she's really mad at me. Not just because of you, but because I won't . . . well, I won't join her coven. She's going to try to get revenge, and one way she does that might be . . . well, she might try to tell you some things about me—"

"What kind of things?" Zach asked, a little too quickly.

My cheeks began to heat up, but I kept my gaze on the game.

"Stuff about me being a witch," I said. "I'm not, but, like I said . . . I used to be into that stuff. And she might say some stuff about . . . well, a guy—"

"The guy who was stalking you," Zach finished for me. "Yeah, I figured. What kind of stuff about him?"

"I don't know," I said. "Whatever she says about him will be a lie, because she doesn't know the whole story."

"What *is* the whole story?" Zach asked. "Jean, what

happened with this guy? What did he do to you, that you had to flee halfway across the country?"

I threw him a startled glance. "He didn't do anything to me. It wasn't like that at all. But that's what I mean. She might try to make out—I don't even know. The thing is, Zach, Tory's got problems." I thought about Petra's picture at the bottom of that litter box. "*Serious* problems."

"I know she has problems," Zach said. "My God, Jean, she hung a headless rat from your locker door. This is not the mark of someone who's got it all together. All the more reason for someone to tell her parents."

"Zach, it won't do any good. She'll just deny it. And there's no proof it was her—"

The shrill blast of a whistle interrupted us. Coach Winthrop bellowed, "Rosen! Honeychurch! This isn't the student lounge. Get up!"

I climbed hurriedly to my feet.

"Please, Zach," I said, feeling sick to my stomach. "Let me handle it, okay? I know everything is going to be all right."

He shook his head. "You *know* it? As in you've looked into the future and seen it?"

I grimaced. "Well, no . . . not exactly. But things can't get any worse, can they?"

CHAPTER THIRTEEN

And for the rest of the week, things didn't—get any worse, anyway. Nothing bad happened. Tory was being kept pretty busy by her parents, who had finally been alerted to the fact that she was flunking out of most of her classes, due almost entirely to the fact that she hadn't done a lick of homework all semester. How could she? She'd been out almost every night with Gretchen and Lindsey, playing at being witches.

But my aunt and uncle finally put a stop to that, by canceling all of their social engagements and staying home to supervise her comings and goings, and by hiring Tory a tutor, whom she was forced to see six days a week, including Saturday mornings. Tory put up an enormous fight, but her parents weren't backing down.

Personally, I took this as a pretty good sign that things might actually calm down.

Zach, however, was dubious.

"I've seen it before," he said, with a shrug, when I told him about it. "Your aunt and uncle get in her face about her grades for a while—get her to see her therapist more regularly, the works—and then she'll do something dramatic to make them feel guilty, and they'll back off."

I found this hard to believe, but Zach, who still wanted to tell Aunt Evelyn and Uncle Ted about the rat—except I wouldn't let him—only said, "Just you wait. You'll see."

I did wait, thinking that he'd be proved wrong. Aunt Evelyn remained vigilant for the rest of the week about checking with Tory's teachers to find out what her homework was, and Uncle Ted went over it with her every night, even after she'd met with the tutor. Except for the dirty looks she regularly shot me, Tory left me alone . . . and I didn't think it was because of the pentacle I was wearing for protection, either. She left Petra alone, too. Was that because of the binding spell?

Or had Tory really turned over a new leaf?

"I think she's doing better," I told Zach, over dinner at a boisterous Italian restaurant the night we went to see Nigel Kennedy. "She doesn't have time to think up ways to torture people. She's too busy catching up with her Geometry homework."

"Well, maybe she hasn't strung any more dead animals from your locker," Zach said, "but that doesn't mean she doesn't plan on doing something worse. That girl has it in for you, Jean."

But, giddy with joy at being out on the town with

Zach—even if we did spend a good portion of the meal discussing Willem's impending visit, and how that would impact Zach's campaign to win the heart of the woman of his dreams—I couldn't exactly share his gloom over Tory.

And by the end of the concert, he was smiling as much as I was . . . though probably more in amusement over how hard I'd clapped than because of anything else. It wasn't until we were strolling home, having decided to walk in order to enjoy the warm night air, that anything happened to dampen my spirits.

"It wasn't the most boring concert I've ever been to," Zach was trying to assure me.

"Then why were your eyes closed during most of it?"

"I was resting them," Zach said. "Honest. Seriously, I have nothing against classical music. Jazz, though? Don't get me started on jazz. Especially—what's it called? Free jazz. You ever try tapping your foot to free jazz? Yeah, not gonna happen. What I really like is the blues. There's a great blues place downtown . . . maybe we should go there next weekend. I have to get you a fake ID first, since they don't let you in if you're under twenty-one."

"That'd be great," I said.

"Actually," Zach said, "we better make it the weekend after next. Next weekend is the spring dance. You know, the formal. I don't know if you'd want to go—it's pretty lame. But I've never been, so I thought, well . . . would you want to go? With me? To the dance? Strictly as friends, of course."

My grin felt as if it might split my head in two. It's true he was in love with another girl. But he'd asked me, not her, to the dance.

This was too good to be true. This couldn't be happening to me, Jinx Honeychurch. This had to be happening to some other girl.

"Okay," I said, my heart feeling as if it were about to burst. "That sounds like it might be fun. . . ."

And then we turned the corner onto East Sixty-ninth Street.

And I was able to see the ambulance parked in front of the Gardiners' townhouse, the flashing red lights reflected off all the dark windows in the brownstones around it.

"It's probably nothing," Zach called after me, as I broke into a run.

It wasn't nothing, though. We got there just as the paramedics emerged, bearing Tory on a stretcher. I saw at once that she was conscious, and even looking around. When her gaze fell upon me and Zach, her eyes, as dramatically made up as ever, narrowed dangerously. And then they were loading her into the back of the ambulance, and I couldn't see her anymore, because they'd closed the doors.

I raced up the stoop and nearly collided with Petra, who was standing in the foyer, flipping through a pile of credit cards while a police officer stood nearby.

"Oh, Jean," she cried, her pretty face tear-stained. "Oh, Jean, thank goodness you are home. You will stay here with the children, while I go with Torrance? Her parents—they had a benefit to attend. They aren't here. She was doing so much better, they thought it would be all right to go out—"

I said, "Of course." It was Zach, who'd raced in behind me, who asked Petra, "What happened?"

"It was my fault," Petra said, as she thumbed through the pile of plastic cards. "I was supposed to check on her at six o'clock, but I was too busy helping Jean get ready to go out—"

I slid a guilty look in Zach's direction. Petra *had* spent nearly an hour helping me put together an outfit for my date with Zach at six, instead of checking on Tory, who was supposed to be in her room studying.

"If I had checked her then," Petra said, her voice filled with barely suppressed tears, "I would have found her sooner. But with helping you, and then Zach coming over, and then getting the children's dinner, and then their baths, and storytime—I just forgot. She was so quiet, I forgot she was even home. When has she ever been home before on a Saturday night? Oh!" She turned to the police officer. "I can't find it!"

"That's all right, miss," the police officer said. "Just take them all, and you can look for it on your way to the hospital."

"The insurance card," Petra explained to me, as she slipped out the door. "I can't find it. I haven't had a chance to call Mr. and Mrs. Gardiner, either. Can you call them, Jean? Tell them we're at—" She threw a questioning glance at the police officer, who said, "Cabrini."

"Cabrini Hospital," Petra repeated, as she started down the front steps toward the waiting ambulance. "Will you tell them to meet me there, Jean? Tell them Torrance—"

"Torrance *what*?" I asked, my voice breaking.

"Tried to kill herself," Petra called, holding up the tiny clear plastic bag Shawn had delivered Tory's Valium in. "Overdose."

"Oh," I said, looking from the plastic bag to Petra to the cop and then back again. "Actually, if the pills were in that bag, they were just baby aspirin."

CHAPTER FOURTEEN

Well, what else was I supposed to do?

I couldn't just let my own cousin go around taking drugs. Not if there was something I could do to stop her.

So I'd found her secret stash one night when she wasn't home (it hadn't been that hard; she'd hidden the pills inside her jewelry box), then searched all over the local Duane Reade until I found similar-looking, but harmless, pills that I could substitute in place of the real thing—which I'd then flushed down the toilet.

"When she gets home," Zach observed, over his Coke, "she's going to kill you."

"She was going to kill me before this," I said glumly. "All this will do is cement her resolve."

"You know she didn't really mean to do it, anyway," Zach said. He lifted the soda can to his lips and took a long swallow.

"Didn't mean to do it? Zach, of course she did. You

don't overdose on Valium by accident. That's just crazy!"

"Huh." Zach reached into the bag of chips someone had left open on the kitchen table, and helped himself to a handful. "Crazy like a fox. Valium's the one drug it's pretty hard to kill yourself with. And her timing was impeccable, in case you haven't noticed."

Slumped miserably in the chair at which Alice usually sat at breakfast time, I glanced at Zach in astonishment. "Her timing? What are you talking about?"

"She knew you and I were going out tonight, right?"

I chewed my lip, remembering our confrontation in the kitchen.

"Well," I said. "Yes."

"That's what I thought. So she must've taken the pills at suppertime," he said. "Right before I came to pick you up. If Petra had checked on her, like she was supposed to, she would have found Tory sprawled across the floor, and our little trip to the theater"—he bit down noisily on a chip—"would have been indefinitely postponed."

I stared at him across the kitchen table. "You can't be serious," I said. "You're saying Tory wasn't trying to kill herself at all—that she took a handful of pills just to keep me from going out with you?"

He shrugged and washed the chip down with a swig of soda.

"Not a handful," he said. "Two. That's how many she told the paramedics she'd taken. Tory knows two Valiums won't do anything. It's all just for show. A big, inconvenient show. She'd never really hurt herself. Fortunately for us, this time, you swapped out the real thing for some baby aspirin. And then Petra screwed up, and didn't find Tory until after we'd left."

"Oh, Zach." I sighed. "Poor Petra thinks this was all her fault, but it isn't. It was mine."

Zach put his soda can down with a thump. "Screw that," he said, making a face.

But it was easy for Zach to say screw that. It wasn't so easy to say it myself. Tory had, after all, confided in me, showing me that doll she'd made. And how had I paid her back? By going out with Zach myself. Sure, Zach didn't like me—not the way I liked him, anyway. We were just friends.

But he and Tory were just friends, and he wasn't going to any concerts with her. Of course she'd been jealous. Of course she'd acted out of that jealousy.

And now he'd asked me to the dance. If she'd tried to kill herself—or, if you believed Zach, faked a suicide attempt—just because we'd gone to a concert together, what would she do when she learned Zach had asked me to the spring formal?

I didn't know. But I did know I didn't want to find out.

It was right then that the phone rang. I was up and out from behind the table, snatching the phone from its cradle, before it rang a second time.

"It's me," Aunt Evelyn said. "We're here at the hospital with Tory. We'll be home soon. She's going to be fine. Thanks to you."

148

I let out a gusty sigh of relief. "Thank goodness." I gave Zach a thumbs-up signal. He mouthed, *I told you so.*

"How are the kids?" Aunt Evelyn asked.

"Asleep," I said. Alice had mercifully never woken up. Teddy had heard the commotion and come downstairs, but Zach had convinced him to go back to bed by promising a game of catch in the garden the next day.

"Good. Well, it looks like they're going to discharge her soon. They didn't have to pump her stomach, once they knew it was . . . well, what you said. I could hardly believe it when they told me—I don't know how she got hold of *Valium*. How did you know, Jean?"

"Know what?"

"Know that she had those pills?"

I swallowed and said, "I, um, just found them—"

"And didn't tell us?" Aunt Evelyn sounded really disappointed in me. "I'm very grateful for what you did do, Jean, but you still should have told us. Tory is—Oh, here comes the doctor. Don't wait up for us, Jean. We'll talk in the morning. Thank you for watching the kids."

"Oh, it's no pro—"

But Aunt Evelyn had already hung up.

I put down the receiver, then turned toward Zach. I felt as if I were going to be sick. But I had no choice.

Tory had seen to that.

"So?" Zach was looking at me with those intense green eyes. "She's okay, right? I told you so."

149

"She's fine," I said. And swallowed. "Zach. I can't go to the dance with you." I said it fast. And I said it firmly.

He just went on looking at me.

"That's what she wants, you know," he said. "That's why she did it."

"Still," I said, remembering how ragged Aunt Evelyn's voice sounded on the phone. "I can't go. I'm sorry."

Zach rolled his eyes. "Stop beating yourself up. None of this is your fault."

"It is too my fault! That's why I can't go with you. It wouldn't be right. You'd better ask someone else."

Zach looked angry. "I don't *want* to ask anyone else," he said. "If I can't go with the girl I want, I won't go with anyone."

"Why?" I demanded hotly. "Petra's the one you want, but you were going with me. So what difference does it make?"

"You know what?" he said, letting out a sudden—and totally humorless—laugh. "You're right. It doesn't make any difference at all. I'm going home now. I'll see you tomorrow."

And then he was gone.

I was all alone in the Gardiners' kitchen. Which made it easy to do what I did next, which was sit down and cry my eyes out for a good ten minutes. I wasn't just crying for myself, either, or because I'd lost Zach—not that I'd ever had him in the first place.

No, I was crying for Tory, and for Petra, and for all

the people my magic—was it magic, or was it just simply bad luck?—had hurt.

Because, in the end, wasn't what Tory had done to herself a direct result of my binding spell? I'd bound her from harming others . . .

. . . but not from hurting herself.

This fact stung all the more when she finally got home, and I saw her there with them—her parents and Petra—in the foyer when I hurried in to greet them. She was pale, and looked thinner than ever.

But though she might have looked wan, there was nothing weak about the way that she flung a look of pure, unadulterated malevolence over her shoulder as she paused on her way up the staircase, upon hearing my voice when I said, "Oh, you're home."

"Oh, Jean," Aunt Evelyn said, as she shrugged off her evening coat. "You're still up? You didn't have to wait. It's late."

"I was too worried to sleep," I said.

"Well, you don't have to worry anymore," Uncle Ted said, glancing up at Tory on the stairs. "She's fine. Thanks to you."

Hearing this, Tory's face lost some of its paleness and turned a sort of mottled red color. Then, looking down at me, she spat, "I will get you for this if it's the last thing I do, Jinx!"

"Tory!" Uncle Ted looked appalled. "Your cousin might possibly have saved your life tonight. The appropriate thing to do would be to thank her."

"Oh, I'll thank her, all right," Tory said, with a sneer. "I have a very special thank-you I've been saving up, just for Jinx."

"Torrance!" Aunt Evelyn's voice was so hard, it could have cut glass. "Go to your room. We will discuss this in the morning. *With* your therapist."

Tory shot me one last baleful glare, then ran up the stairs. When her door had slammed, Petra, who'd been standing quietly by the French doors to the living room, said, "Well. I'm tired. If it is all right with you, I think I will go to bed."

"Oh, of course, Petra," Aunt Evelyn said in an entirely different tone. "Thank you so much for everything you did tonight."

"It was no problem," Petra said. "I'm just glad that . . . well. I'm just glad. Good night."

She vanished through the door that led to her cozy basement apartment. As soon as she was gone, I turned to Aunt Evelyn and Uncle Ted.

It was time. I'd done it with Zach. Now it was their turn.

I didn't want to. But I didn't have a choice.

"I know you're both tired and probably want to go to bed," I said. "But I just wanted to say that I'm sorry I didn't tell you about the drugs. That I knew Tory had them, I mean. And . . . and . . ." I added this last part in a rush, having rehearsed it virtually nonstop in my head since seeing Tory being carried out of the house on that stretcher.

"And if you want to send me home, I totally understand."

Both Aunt Evelyn and Uncle Ted stared down at me as if I'd suggested they lop off my head.

"Send you home?" Uncle Ted echoed. "Why would we do that?"

"Oh, Jean, honey." Aunt Evelyn, smelling as exotic as always, and looking beautiful in a long, black evening sheath, put an arm around me. "What happened tonight wasn't your fault. Tory's been having . . . difficulties . . . for some time now. I'm sorry I lashed out at you on the phone. I was just upset. But we don't blame you. Not at all."

"But"—how could I explain this without making Tory hate me (not that she didn't already) forever if she found out about it?—"it's just that . . . well, this thing with Zach—"

Aunt Evelyn's pretty face hardened, and she dropped her arm from me. But not, as I first thought, because she was angry with me.

"Is that what this is all about?" she asked. "We wondered. Tory's had a crush on him for quite a while. It's unfortunate he doesn't return her feelings, but I've explained to her . . . that's life. It isn't your fault he chose you and not her."

I blushed to the roots of my hair.

"Oh, no," I said, horrified. "Zach and I . . . we aren't going out. We're just friends. I don't know why Tory thinks it's anything more than that."

Aunt Evelyn raised her eyebrows. "Really?" she said. "Well, maybe because he always seems to be—"

But she didn't get to finish, because Uncle Ted interrupted.

"Wait. I can't keep up. I thought Tory had moved on from Zach," Uncle Ted said. "What about this Shawn guy?"

"They're just friends, I think," Aunt Evelyn said.

Yeah. Friends with benefits.

"The thing is," I said, feeling as if the point of my speech had been lost somehow, "I think my being friends with Zach is what made Tory do what she did. So maybe if I just went home—"

"You can't go back to Hancock yet, Jean," Aunt Evelyn said, looking troubled. "Ted and I love having you here. And Teddy and Alice adore you. Petra can't say enough good things about you. Even Marta says you're like a breath of fresh air through the house. You've become such a fixture here, I don't know what we'd do without you."

"And," added Uncle Ted, "frankly, I think your being here has been good for Tory. I know tonight was rough. But imagine how much worse it might have been, if you hadn't . . . well, done what you did."

"You set a good example for her, Jean," Aunt Evelyn agreed. "You've got your feet planted so firmly on the ground. I have to admit, Jean, I was really hoping some of your good influence might rub off on Tory."

I bit my lower lip. A good example? They were hoping some of my good influence might rub off on Tory? God, no wonder she hated me so much! *I* hated me, hearing myself described in such a way.

But the truth was, I didn't want to leave. Even if Aunt Evelyn was totally off the mark with her whole "feet planted so firmly on the ground" comment. She clearly didn't have any idea where I was headed tomorrow— where I knew that, now that I was staying, I had no choice but to head.

And I wasn't about to tell her.

"All right," I said. "I'll stay."

After all, what was the worst that could happen? Nothing as bad as what had happened back in Hancock.

Or so I thought. Then.

CHAPTER FIFTEEN

The chimes over the shop door tinkled as I walked in. The woman behind the counter looked up from the book she was reading and said, "Blessings—"

Then she recognized me, and her face broke into a smile. "Oh, it's you," she said kindly. "How are you, sister?"

I approached the counter tentatively. I'd come alone this time, maneuvering the New York City transit system without Zach's help. It had been scary, taking the train by myself—especially when the subway cars came thundering into the station, roaring so loudly I could hear nothing else.

But I'd done it. And now I stood in the shop on Ninth Street, feeling like I'd been foolish to come. Magic couldn't help me.

And neither could this woman.

No one could help me.

The woman put down her book. I glanced at the

cover. It wasn't, as I might have expected, a book on witchcraft, but a plain old science-fiction novel.

"What is it, sweetheart?" the woman asked in a sympathetic voice.

I looked around. Except for the cat, who lay on a pile of books in the corner, busily washing herself, there was no one else in the store. I swallowed. I felt ridiculous. And yet . . .

"Someone I know is casting a spell," I said, in a rush. After all . . . what could it hurt? It might even help. "All I know about it is that one of the ingredients is some kind of fungus that grows on headstones, and the, um, person who is casting the spell had to collect the fungus at midnight, under a waxing moon. I was wondering if you had any idea what kind of spell that might be."

The woman, who looked to be in her thirties, with perfect skin and long, dark hair, knit her brow thoughtfully. I was worried she was getting ready to give a speech about how the practice of witchcraft was really all about empowerment, and that spells were just a witch's way of focusing her energy on solving a certain problem, when instead, the woman said, "Well, a waxing moon is when the moon is getting fuller, so a spell done in that period would indicate growth of some kind. It's a good time for new beginnings."

"So . . . it could be a good spell, then?" I brightened. "I mean, new beginnings are good, right?"

"Not always," the saleslady said, looking at me sympathetically. "Is this person angry, by any chance?"

I swallowed again. *I have a very special thank-you I've been saving up, just for Jinx.* "Yes."

She nodded and said, "That's a problem, then. But nothing you shouldn't be able to handle."

I gaped at her. *"Me?* Hardly."

The woman looked amused.

"I can tell just by looking at you that you're a natural witch . . . and powerful, too, I sense," she said.

I shook my head so hard my curls slapped my cheeks. "No. No, you don't understand. Any power I have . . . it's bad. Everything I touch gets messed up. That's why they call me Jinx."

The woman smiled, but at the same time, shook her head. "You're not jinxed," she said. "But I do sense . . . pardon me for saying it, but I do sense that you fear it. Your power."

I couldn't help staring. How did she—

Oh. Right. She was a witch.

"I cast a spell once," I said, my throat suddenly very dry. "My first spell. My only spell, really, except a binding spell. That spell—my first one . . . it went wrong. Really, really wrong."

"Ah." She nodded knowingly. "Now I see. It frightened you, this power you discovered in yourself. That might be what's causing your so-called bad luck. You're bringing it on yourself, through your fear."

What? I was causing my bad luck? Impossible. Why would I do *that?*

"I understand how it must be for you," she went on

158

sympathetically. "And you're right to be cautious. A power as strong as yours . . . it *is* a lot of responsibility. You should never use it lightly. And never, as I'm sure you learned, to manipulate the will of another. Because it could go wrong . . . badly wrong, as your first spell seemed to. But that doesn't mean you should be frightened of it. Careful, yes. Frightened, no. Because your power—your gift—is a part of you. A good part, not a bad part. By not embracing it, you are denying a part of yourself. It's like saying you don't like yourself. And that's wrong. Surely you can see that's what's happening, why you have a sort of . . . well, as you put it, jinx?"

I found myself nodding. I didn't trust myself to speak.

"The magic you possess," the woman went on gently, "is very old, and very strong. I would guess that whoever it is that is casting this spell against you—the one with the mushrooms—she doesn't have the slightest idea what she's up against. You will defeat her . . . but not unless you embrace that which you fear."

Embrace what I feared? She had to be kidding. I mean, it was easy for *her* to say. Maybe if she walked around in my shoes for a day—just a day—she'd see there wasn't anything to embrace . . . only stuff to run from, screaming. Headless rats and bike messengers reeling out of control and dolls with pins in their heads and . . .

The woman smiled at me. "You don't believe me," she said. "I see that. And I don't mind. But this binding spell of yours—did it work?"

I thought about Petra . . . and Willem winning that

trip to New York, and her A in her Glyconutrition class.

"Y-yes," I said hesitantly. "Actually, it seems to have worked. So far."

"You weren't frightened of your power then, were you?"

"No," I said. "I was angry."

"See? Anger can be healthy. When the time comes—and it *will* come—remember that. And what I said. Embrace your powers—love yourself the way Nature made you, and you will prevail. Always."

I *wanted* to believe her. But how could I embrace something that for my whole life had just been screwing things up for me? It was impossible.

Still, to be polite, I smiled.

"Um," I said, "the thing is, I'm not so worried about myself. I'm more concerned about . . . about a friend of mine." I didn't want to admit out loud that I was afraid Tory was going to try to do something to hurt Zach. Not on purpose, of course—but I couldn't get the picture of that doll with the pin in its head out of my mind's eye. I knew—only too well—how a spell could backfire and end up hurting the one person the caster never meant to harm. "I'm worried this . . . person . . . who's doing the spell with the mushrooms might try to do something to him. I was hoping you might have something here that could protect him . . . without his being aware of it, if possible."

"He's not a believer?" the woman asked, with a wry smile.

"Um . . . not exactly."

The woman's blue eyes crinkled. "I see," she said. "Well, as a matter of fact . . ."

And then the woman—who really was, I realized by now, an honest-to-goodness, practicing witch, although she wasn't wearing a stitch of black, just a Wonder Bread T-shirt and blue jeans—slipped off her stool and came out from behind the counter.

"A little bit of powdered lemon rind," she said, going to the far wall of the shop. It was lined with shelves, upon which were the kind of glass jars with the metal lids you lifted up to get at what was inside, like in an old-fashioned candy store. "That's for cleansing." She lifted a lid and spooned out a little bit of yellow powder into a small cloth bag. "Then some ginger, for energy." She added a few slivers of a root to the bag. "Clove, for protection, of course—" A few sticks went into the bag. "And let's not forget a little rosemary." She turned and winked at me. "For love, as in 'love thine enemy,' impossible as that might seem at the moment. There." She gave the top of the sack a twist, then tied it closed with a bit of red ribbon. "With luck, any spell that is cast against him," she said, handing the bag over to me, "will bounce harmlessly off, and end up right back at the caster, as long as he carries this."

With luck. I swallowed and took the bag. "Kind of like that thing you say when you're a kid? 'I'm rubber, you're glue, anything you say bounces off me and sticks to you'?"

The woman laughed, her blue eyes crinkling at the

corners again. "Exactly like that."

I opened my backpack, and put the fragrant-smelling sachet inside it, wondering how on earth I was going to sneak it onto Zach's person without his knowing it . . . especially considering the fact that he didn't seem to be speaking to me at the moment. "Well, thanks a lot."

I failed, however, to see how a bunch of dried herbs was going to protect anyone from Tory's wrath.

On the other hand, I had once failed to see how a different spell was going to work, and look where it had landed me.

"How much do I owe you?"

The witch laughed. "Nothing! It's my pleasure to help you. I'm Lisa, by the way."

"Jean," I said, reaching out to shake the witch's hand. "But you're going to go out of business if you keep giving me things. You already gave me this." I touched the pentacle at my neck. "Remember?"

Lisa smiled. "I remember. Wear it in good health. Come back in a few days, and let me know how everything turns out."

I shouldered my backpack again and said, "Well, all right. Thank you."

"And don't forget," Lisa said, as I was leaving. "Embrace your gift, Jean. Never fear it. It's a part of who you are, after all."

I nodded and left the store after thanking her again. There was a part of me, of course, that thought the whole thing was silly. Embrace my gift? Surely she couldn't mean the gift Great-Great-And-So-On-Grandmother Branwen had left me . . . or us, if you wanted to include Tory. The gift about which Tory had said, so mockingly, that she wasn't afraid to use, though I might be. The gift of magic. How could that woman have even known about Branwen, let alone her gift?

Did I have some kind of power—really and truly—as the lady seemed to think?

And was I really causing my own bad luck, by fearing and not embracing it?

There was only one way to find out.

CHAPTER SIXTEEN

I may have chronically bad luck—possibly brought on by my own insecurities—but I'm not dumb. I wasn't about to tell Tory's parents where she'd gotten the drugs. I was having a hard enough time fitting in at my school—considering the headless rat showing up on my locker door, and the rumors about my stalker back home—without also being labeled a narc.

So how Shawn ended up getting expelled, it had nothing to do with me.

When, during third period on Monday morning, word went around that school administrators were searching people's lockers, I didn't think anything of it.

But when, during fourth period (U.S. History, which I happened to have with both Tory and Shawn, though Tory wasn't in school on Monday, due to having to go to follow-up appointments with both her therapist and her doctor), the principal actually showed up at the classroom door and said to Mrs. Tyler, "May I see Shawn Kettering, please?" even I knew it wasn't a good sign.

Then, at lunch, word got out he was gone. Booted. Done.

"Well, I for one am glad." Chanelle was philosophical about the whole thing as she licked the filling from her Devil Dog. "Like, Robert will have a much harder time getting hold of it now. You know. Weed. Sure, he could go down to Washington Square to buy it. But half those dealers are undercover cops. He won't risk it. If he gets busted, his parents'll kill him. Now maybe he'll even be straight for the formal. That'll be a change."

"I'm gonna have to be straight for the formal?" Robert actually looked a little queasy. "Dude, that's just not right."

"Oh, get over yourself," Chanelle said. "It'll be good for you to see how the rest of us live."

"How the rest of you live sucks," Robert said.

I was laughing over his chagrin when a familiar, gravelly voice very close to my ear went, "Laugh it up, NARC."

I nearly choked on my chicken finger. I turned in my seat to see Gretchen and Lindsey scowling down at me.

"Are you happy now, narc?" Gretchen wanted to know. "Like it wasn't good enough to steal Zach out from under Torrance's nose? You had to get her boyfriend Shawn booted from school, too?"

I stared up at the two girls. "I didn't steal Zach from anyone," I said, when I finally found my voice. "He and I aren't going out. And I don't know what you're talking about, with Shawn. It wasn't me who told."

"Oh, right," Lindsey said, making a face. "Preacher's daughter? Of course it was you."

"It *wasn't*," I said.

"Whatever you say, *narc*," Gretchen said. And then she and Lindsey took their trays and headed toward the far side of the cafeteria.

When I turned, distressed, back to the table, Chanelle was wearing a sympathetic expression.

"Oh, Jean," she said. "Don't let those witches get you down. We know it wasn't you. And even if it was, who could blame you, after what happened to Torrance?"

Because, of course, news of Tory's suicide attempt had spread like wildfire across the school—though I hadn't said a word about it.

"It *wasn't* me," I said fiercely.

"Don't worry about it." Robert look bored. "No one listens to those two skanks anyway."

But he was wrong. Either that, or Gretchen and Lindsey weren't the only two going around saying I was the one who'd told on Shawn. Everywhere I went, people started whispering, and only stopped when I looked their way. By the time fifth period P.E. rolled around, I had taken about all I could handle.

There was only one other person at Chapman whose reaction to the Shawn thing I cared about. And he'd been avoiding me like the plague since Saturday night. I hadn't been near enough to Zach to exchange a single word with him, let alone slip Lisa's sachet into his backpack.

Not that I blamed him. Between my troubles with Tory, and then the witch thing—and now this—I must have seemed like the great big bad-luck magnet I knew myself, in actual fact, to be.

Coach Winthrop had us doing softball again. It was no miracle that Zach and I ended up on the same team. Coach Winthrop, in a rare moment of good humor, apparently decided it would be hilarious to appoint a music geek—and rumored narc, although I'm pretty sure the coach didn't know about that yet—like me a team captain. Zach was, of course, the first person I chose for my team. Hey, it might turn out to be the only way I'd ever get him to talk to me.

But in the end, I was wrong. Again. He came over and spoke to me of his own free will while we were waiting for our turns at bat.

"So, Cousin Jean from Iowa," he said. "You weren't lying when you said you have chronic bad luck. You seriously have the worst luck of anyone I've ever met. Now you're a narc, I hear?"

It was all I could do—seriously—not to burst into tears right there behind the chain-link fence, even though we all know there's no crying in baseball. Or softball, either.

"It wasn't me," I said, a little too loudly. Everyone else on our team looked over at me.

Zach's smile was gentle. "Relax, Jean," he said. "I know it wasn't you. Interesting that that's what the rumor should be, though, huh?"

"It makes sense," I said with a shrug. "I mean, she's

my cousin. I'm new here. I'm—"

"—a preacher's daughter," Zach said. "Yeah, I know. I heard them all, too. So. What are you going to do?"

I shrugged again. "What *can* I do?"

"You can go to the dance with me," Zach said.

I looked up at him owlishly. "Are you crazy? That'll just make things worse. Gretchen and Lindsey are already going around saying—"

"Exactly," Zach said. "Gretchen and Lindsey are the ones feeding fuel to the fire. And why do you think they're doing that?"

Because I won't join forces with Tory and help them to become the most powerful coven on the eastern seaboard. Only I couldn't say that. So I said, "Because they hate me."

"Right. But why do they hate you? Because Tory told them to."

I shook my head, confused. "Are you saying Tory told them I was the one who got Shawn expelled?"

"Does that seem so out of the realm of the possible, given what you know about your cousin?"

I thought about it. I really did. I just couldn't see Tory doing something *that* underhanded. Faking a suicide attempt—given that she was such a drama queen—yes. But spreading a rumor she knew wasn't true about me?

On the other hand, she HAD been IMing an awful lot lately. . . .

Still.

"I don't know, Zach," I said. "I don't think even Tory would stoop that low."

"Fine," he said. "But just in case you change your mind . . . the invitation still stands."

"The invitation . . . to the *dance?*" I'm sorry to say that my voice rose to a squeal at the end.

"Yeah," Zach said, looking bemused, I guess by the squeal. "That one."

"But—" The truth was, though I had said the words two nights ago—the ones telling him I couldn't go to the dance with him—they still hurt . . . they hurt even more than my offer to Tory's parents to go back to Hancock.

But I knew I couldn't hold him to an invitation that he might regret having made. I mean, that wouldn't be fair. No one—not even a guy as great as Zach—wants to associate with a rumored narc.

"Seriously, Zach," I said. "It's all right. You can take someone else. I won't mind." It would kill me. But I wasn't going to let him know that.

But to my surprise, instead of arguing some more, he said, "Look, you're taking U.S. History. Has Mrs. Tyler gotten to the different styles of government yet?"

"Yes," I said, wondering what on earth this had to do with the dance.

"Has she gotten to the laissez-faire approach of governing . . . of letting things take their own course?"

"Abstention by the government from interfering with the free market," I said.

"Right. I guess you could say I have always taken a sort of laissez-faire approach to Tory. As long as she didn't bug me, I wasn't going to bug her, know what I mean? I suspected for a while that she had a crush on me, but—"

"But you liked Petra," I finished for him. "And so long as you remained on friendly terms with Tory, you had an excuse to see her. Petra, I mean."

He actually looked embarrassed.

"Well," he said. "Yeah. Basically. For a while, anyway. But here's the thing: I don't plan on taking the laissez-faire approach to Tory anymore . . . or anyone else for that matter. I think it's time I took a stand."

I said carefully, "But Zach, if you and I go to the dance, and Tory gets mad, and then I"—I swallowed, but carried on—"I go back to Hancock, you won't have an excuse to see Petra anymore. Tory won't forgive you, you know."

"I know," Zach said. "That's what I'm trying to say. I'm prepared to make that sacrifice."

I looked at him curiously. "But why? Why would you do that? Don't you love Petra anymore?"

Zach had the strangest look on his face. It seemed to be halfway between frustration and amusement. He opened his mouth to say something in reply, only to be interrupted by Coach Winthrop, who bellowed, "Rosen! You're up!"

Giving me an apologetic smile, Zach went off to grab a bat.

I leaned back against the bench, wondering what he

could possibly have been about to say. Could Zach's feelings for Petra have changed? Had seeing her so excited about Willem's impending visit finally made him realize he really never had a chance with her?

What was going on?

I never got the chance to find out, though, because later in the game, someone hit a pop fly that collided with my head (typical) and I had to sit on the sidelines until Coach Winthrop was finally convinced I didn't have a concussion and let me go back to the locker room to change.

But if Zach's feelings for Petra were history, they weren't the only ones, I discovered when I got home from school that day. So, it turned out, were Tory's feelings for me. Her feelings of animosity toward me, anyway.

Or so she claimed.

I was in my room practicing when I heard the tap on my door.

"Come in," I said, lowering my violin. I knew it had to be something important. I had drilled it into Teddy's and Alice's heads that during my hour-long practice every afternoon, I wasn't to be disturbed, no matter what had just happened on *SpongeBob*.

I should have known it couldn't have been either of the younger Gardiners, who really were good about not bothering me when they heard Stravinsky coming out of my room. Instead, it was Tory.

"Hey," she said to me, after closing the door behind

her and leaning against it. "Got a minute?"

I stared at her. There was something . . . different about her. Really different. At first I couldn't put my finger on just what exactly.

Then it hit me. She wasn't dressed in black. She had on jeans—ordinary ones, not the ones she sometimes wore that she'd decorated all over with ankhs and pentacles in black Magic Marker.

And she wasn't wearing a ton of makeup, either. An incredibly striking-looking girl, Tory had never needed all the eyeliner and mascara she slathered on, anyway. Without it, she looked just as pretty . . . only in a different, more vulnerable way.

Something else was different, too. It took me another minute to realize what, but then it hit me. She wasn't glaring at me. She actually looked . . . well, as if she were glad to see me.

"I just wanted to apologize," she said, "for the way I've been treating you since you got here."

I nearly dropped my violin, I was so astonished.

"I know I've been a real pscyho lately," Tory went on. "I don't know what's been the matter with me. I guess it just all got to be too much—school, and the pressure to be popular, and the thing with Zach, and . . . and the witch thing. And I ended up taking it out on you. Which isn't fair. I realize that now. My therapist—you know, the one I've been seeing—has really been helping me with that. So I just wanted to say I'm sorry for the way I've been acting, and thank you for what you did the other night—with the drugs, and all. I know you just did it because you were worried about me. I'm lucky to have so many people in my life who care about me so much. That's been a real wake-up call for me. So . . . thanks, Jinx. And . . . if it's okay with you . . . I'd like you to give me another chance."

I couldn't stop staring at her. I've heard of therapy working miracles, but I'd never expected anything like this.

"I . . ." What could I say? I was thrilled to have the old Tory—the one from five years ago—back. If it was really true. "Oh, Tory. Do you really mean it?"

"Of course I mean it," Tory said, with a smile. Even her hair looked different. She had pinned it up, out of her eyes, so that she looked almost . . . well, preppy. And happy, for a change. "And I don't want to play at being witches anymore, either. That whole thing about Grandma, and Branwen . . . that was just silly. So was the stuff with Zach, and the doll—" She heaved a shudder. "God! I can't believe I ever did that. It's so embarrassing! I put that stupid doll in the trash and forgot about it, like you said to. I really want us to be friends again, Jinx. Do you think we can?"

"Of course we can," I said. But something was nagging me . . . and it wasn't the tiny knot in my stomach, either. "But what about . . . Shawn?"

"Shawn?" Tory looked confused. Then she laughed. "Oh, Shawn! I know, can you believe that? I can't believe someone turned him in like that. But he'll be all right. I heard his dad already pulled some strings to get him into Spencer. Although Dr. Kettering had to lock up all his prescription pads."

I stared at her. "Your friends—Gretchen and Lindsey— seem to think I did it. The whole *school* seems to think I did it."

"Do they?" Tory shook her head. "But that's just silly! Of course it wasn't you. I can't believe that. God, you really do have the worst luck, Jean. You always did. That's one of the things I love best about you, I guess. You're just so . . . predictable."

I stared at her. She really did seem to be serious. She seemed to be . . . well, the old Tory. She really did.

The next thing I knew, I was walking over to hug her—then realized I was still holding my bow and violin, and, laughing, put them down, then walked into her embrace.

I couldn't believe it! As she hugged me, I had to blink tears from my eyes. It didn't seem possible, but it was really happening. I had the old Tory back!

"Oh, Jean," she said, when we finally let each other go. "I'm so glad you forgive me. Especially when I was so horrible to you."

"Tory." I shook my head. "I'll always forgive you. That's what cousins are for, right? But . . ." It had taken a trip to the hospital to straighten her out, but she seemed genuinely remorseful. Still. "Are you really sure . . . I mean—"

"Oh, Jean, you don't have to worry about me anymore," she said, with a laugh. "I'm really all right. I just hope you won't . . . you know. Feel awkward. Not about the witch thing, but about Zach. I'm really over him. Really. I swear. I don't mind a bit that you two are going out. In fact, I think you make a cute couple. You'll look adorable together at the dance."

"Thanks," I said uncomfortably. "But, like I keep telling you . . . we're not a couple. We're certainly not going to the dance together."

"Why? Didn't he ask you?" Tory's eyes were filled with concern. "That seems weird. I mean, you two have gotten so close . . . even if you are just friends, I'd have thought he'd ask you to the formal. . . ."

"Well," I said awkwardly. "He did. But I said no. Because it just didn't seem like—"

"Oh, Jean!" Tory cried, coming up to me and squeezing my arm. "You guys *have* to go together! You just have to! It won't be the same if you're not there."

"If I'm not . . ." My voice trailed off. "*You're* still going? But I thought—"

"Of course I'm still going! Not with Shawn, of course," she said. "He's not allowed back at any school-sponsored functions. But I thought I would go, you know, stag. Lots of girls do it. I won't look like the biggest freak there by a long shot. And who knows? Maybe I'll find someone there . . . someone a little more interested in being just friends, as opposed to being friends with benefits." She winked at me. "If you know what I mean."

"That's a great idea," I said, thinking it was just the thing Tory needed—a new start, especially in the guy arena. "Wait, I know. Why don't we go together? You and me . . . we can both look for new guys. . . ."

"Oh, no," Tory said. "And leave out poor Zach? That doesn't seem fair. You *have* to go with Zach, Jean. You just have to. If you don't . . . well, I'd feel like it was because of me."

"Well," I said hesitantly.

Tory slapped a hand to her mouth. "Oh, no! It *is* because of me, isn't it? Oh, Jean, I feel awful. Just awful! I don't want my stupid baggage affecting other people. Jean, you've *got* to go with him. You just have to."

"But I already told him I wouldn't," I said, a little helplessly.

"What if you called him and told him you'd changed your mind? I'm sure that he'll still want to go."

"Well," I said again. "I don't know. Maybe. But—"

"Oh, call him," Tory said. She picked up the cordless extension sitting on my bedside table. "Call him right now, and tell him you changed your mind."

"It's not that easy, Tory," I said, thinking of his expression the last time I'd seen him, when I'd asked him if he was still in love with Petra. He'd just looked so *strange*. . . . If he wasn't in love with Petra anymore, what incentive did he have to hang around with me?

None, that's what.

"You'll never know for sure," Tory said, holding the phone out to me, "if you don't even try."

I looked at the phone. She was right, of course. And what could it hurt to ask?

Shrugging, I took the phone from her and punched in Zach's number.

He picked up on the second ring.

"Zach?" I said. "It's me, Jean."

I didn't realize I'd been holding my breath until he said, "Oh, hey," in a voice that indicated that he was actually glad to hear from me. Then I exhaled, all in a rush.

"How's it going?" he asked. "How's your head? I looked for you after class, but you'd already taken off—"

"Yeah, I'm fine now," I said, wincing at this reminder of my truly embarrassing lack of athleticism.

"Good. How's your cousin doing? Has she—"

"Tory's doing great," I interrupted him to say, with a grin in Tory's direction. She grinned back, giving me the thumbs-up for luck. "In fact, that's sort of why I'm calling . . . about the spring formal. The thing is . . . Tory's feeling much, much better today. And she says she'd really hate for us not to go to the dance on her account."

"Oh," Zach said. "She said that, did she?"

"She did," I said. "Actually. So, I was wondering if you still wanted to go." I realized my palms were sweating, and wiped them—transferring the phone from one hand to the other—on my jeans. "With me, I mean."

"Jean," Zach said.

"Yes?"

"Is Tory there in the room with you right now?"

"Uh-huh," I said, careful not to meet Tory's gaze.

"Doesn't this sound like some kind of scam to you?"

"What?" I was startled. "No. No, Zach, it's nothing like that. Tory's going to the dance, too . . . solo, of course, because of what happened to Shawn. And she says she'd feel really bad if we weren't there."

I cleared my throat. This was so awkward. Because if what I think Zach was trying to tell me out on the ball field was really true, he didn't even like Petra that way anymore. So why on earth would he want to keep hanging around with me?

"It's totally fine if you've already found someone else to go with," I added hurriedly. "I was just checking. In case you hadn't. But if you're going with someone else, really, it's fine—"

"It's not that," Zach said. "It's just that you don't think this is all sort of—"

"Jean," Tory said. I glanced at Tory. She was holding out her hand. "Let me talk to him."

Not knowing what else to do, I handed the phone to Tory. She said, in the most animated voice I'd ever heard her use before, "Zach? Hi, it's me, Torrance. Look, Zach, I know this must seem sudden, but I really am so grateful to Jean for what she did for me. I just want her to know how truly sorry I am for the way I've been treating her since she got here, and—what's that? Oh, of *course*, Zach. I already did. And Jean really seems ready to give me another chance. I was hoping you could, too."

There was silence as Tory listened to whatever Zach was saying to her. Then her face broke into a big smile.

"Great," she said. "Thanks, Zach. You won't regret it. Yes. Here she is."

She handed the phone back to me, mouthing, *He said yes!*

I couldn't believe it. Smiling, I put the receiver to my ear. "Zach?"

"She's either a stark raving lunatic, or trying to pull something over on you," Zach said. "But I don't know how we're going to prove either of them. So I say we just go. At least if we're all together, we'll be able to keep an eye on her. Besides, how much trouble could anyone cause at a school dance?"

"True," I said, darting a nervous glance at Tory, worried she might have overheard. But she was looking at the concerto on my music stand, and didn't appear to be paying the slightest bit of attention. "That sounds good. So . . ." I wanted to ask him about what he'd said at the game, about Petra, but I found that I couldn't, with Tory still in the room.

"She still there?" Zach wanted to know.

"Yes," I said.

"Look, I'll talk to you tomorrow at school," he said. "Okay?"

"Okay," I said, relieved. Relieved because I wasn't going to have to bring up the Petra thing after all. Because there was a part of me that really, really didn't want to know. "Bye."

"Bye," Zach said. And hung up.

I put down the phone.

"Well," I said to Tory. "That's that."

"He really did say yes?" Tory asked eagerly.

"He really did," I said.

"Yay!" Tory jumped up and down, clapping her hands, looking so much like her old, former self—the Tory with whom I'd had so much fun, five years ago—that it was impossible to think Zach could be right about her. Maybe he was just being a jaded New Yorker about the whole thing. Maybe Tory really had learned a lesson, and changed her ways.

But I was thinking about what she'd said earlier, about putting the Zach doll she'd made in the trash. Had she really?

Not that I—unlike Zach—didn't believe in her transformation.

But I hadn't been able to get that look she'd given me—Saturday night, on the stairs—out of my head. It was great that she'd had this change of heart, great that she'd given up the witch thing—which, in her case, hadn't been empowering, the way it ought to have been, but more dangerous than anything else.

But what if it *wasn't* true? I mean, what if it was all an act?

I felt AWFUL that I could even think such a thing. I mean, it was so obvious Tory was ready to make a new start. She even asked if she could sit and listen to me practice. I let her, of course—I was much too flattered to say no.

And then, when she'd suggested we go downstairs

and make ourselves hot fudge sundaes and watch some reruns of *The Real World*, well, I hadn't said no to that either.

But later that night, after dinner—the most pleasant meal I'd ever had in the Gardiner household, seeing as how Tory chattered away happily all through it, instead of making sullen comments about everything everyone else said—I stepped out onto the front stoop and skipped down the stairs and onto East Sixty-ninth Street.

Where I started going through the Gardiners' garbage.

It didn't take me long to find it. It was in an *I ♥ New York* shopping bag, all by itself. Tory's Zach doll. She really HAD thrown it away.

She really HAD changed.

And even though she'd said she didn't want to play at being witches anymore, I snuck the Zach doll, in its bag, back inside with me. Not because I didn't trust her—it wasn't that AT ALL. It was just that . . . well, whether Tory had the gift of magic or not, it was still a doll with Zach's hair on it.

And there was no way I was going to let it mold in some landfill out on Staten Island.

I brought the doll into my room and unwrapped it from its plastic bag.

It really was the most horribly made doll I'd ever seen. Still, it was supposed to be Zach. Who knew? Maybe I would give it to him someday (after swearing him to secrecy about where I'd gotten it) for a laugh.

But then, just as I was about to fall asleep that night, something occurred to me. It was stupid, I knew.

But it nevertheless compelled me to get up and pull the doll from the hiding place I'd found for it.

Just as I'd suspected, Tory had left her hair entwined on top of the doll's head with some of Zach's hair.

And I know this was probably the dumbest thing in the world to have done. But I also knew I'd never get back to sleep unless I did it: I carefully separated out all of the strands of Tory's hair, leaving only Zach's on the doll's head, and flushed Tory's down the toilet.

Then I put the doll back where it belonged, and fell into the soundest sleep I'd experienced since moving to New York.

Maybe the lady from Enchantments was right after all:

Everything really was going to be all right.

CHAPTER SEVENTEEN

Willem—Petra's Willem—arrived that Wednesday, bringing with him gifts—a tiny, playable accordion for Alice; an authentic German soccer ball for Teddy; perfume for Tory; catnip for Mouche; a little figurine of a girl playing the violin for me—and a general air of good humor and *joie de vivre*.

He was, of course, devastatingly good-looking. I wouldn't have expected Petra, who was so gorgeous, to date a troll, and she definitely didn't. Willem was even taller than Zach, with blond hair, blue eyes, and a quick, easy grin. I overheard Aunt Evelyn say to my mom, during their weekly phone call, "My God, I'm half in love with him myself."

Petra was, of course, over the moon at having him there.

"He is sleeping on the couch," was what she told Teddy and Alice. And, indeed, there was even a pillow and a blanket folded up on the couch in her snug little basement apartment.

But I still saw the telltale sign of beard burn on her face at breakfast every morning. I wondered how I was going to break the news to Zach that Willem's visit appeared to be going swimmingly—if he even cared anymore. There had never seemed to be a good moment, since that afternoon on the baseball field, to bring up what we'd talked about there—Zach's new, non-laissez-faire policy toward Tory, and how that was going to impact his relationship with Petra . . .

. . . especially since Tory now seemed to be okay with the two of us being friends, and Zach dropped by the house as often as he used to, to play catch with Teddy or hang out in the kitchen with me. (This afforded me ample opportunity to slip Lisa's sachet into his backpack. Not that I didn't believe Tory's claim that she'd given up witchcraft. But I still had Gretchen and Lindsey to worry about. The two of them were throwing me meaner looks than ever every day in the caf . . . especially now that Tory had apologized to Chanelle, as well, and had been forgiven and was eating with me and Chanelle again, and ignoring them.)

I knew I should have come right out and asked Zach, "Are you still in love with Petra?" But every time I thought about doing so, the knot in my stomach—which, since Tory's transformation, had been putting in fewer and fewer appearances—would return in full force.

So I just kept my mouth shut about it. Certainly Zach never brought it up. Although that might have been because he was around enough to see for himself how happy Petra and Willem were together . . .

Not that I had much time to worry about Petra's love life. With the dance coming up in a few days, all of us girls were freaking out over what we were going to wear.

"You have to wear black," Chanelle said.

"Everybody wears black," Tory agreed. "It's like, tradition."

"I don't think my mother would let me wear something black," I said worriedly. My parents, having heard about the dance—but nothing about Tory's suicide attempt (as Aunt Evelyn put it, "God forbid Charlotte should hear about any of that. She'll have you home in a New York second. Maybe it would be best to, er, shield her from the truth.")—had sent fifty dollars to go toward a dress. I wanted the money to stretch as far as possible. Which was why I was planning on heading to H&M on Fifth Avenue.

But Tory, who'd stopped teasing me about my family's relative poverty, seemed appalled at the idea.

"You can't wear a dress from H&M to the formal," she said, shocked. "Everyone will know you only spent fifty bucks on it."

"But that amount of money won't go very far at a regular store," I said, having scanned the dresses at Bloomingdale's and Macy's already.

"Leave it to me," Tory said.

And that day, she came home from her therapist's office with a bag from Betsey Johnson.

"She has a shop next to Dr. Lippman's," Tory explained excitedly, as she pulled a long, slinky gown out of it. "I saw this in the window, and knew it would be perfect for you. Don't worry, it was on sale. More than fifty dollars, but consider it, you know. My official thank-you gift for all you've done for me."

I stared down at the dress. It was beautiful. But . . .

"It's black," I said.

"I know it's black," Tory said, with a hint of her old asperity in her voice. "But look at it. It's perfect for you. With your white skin, and that red hair—"

"But . . . it's black." I looked up at her. "My mom would kill me. She says I'm too young for black. And you know Aunt Evelyn's going to e-mail her pictures . . ."

"Tell your mother to get with the twenty-first century," Tory said with a laugh. "This is Manhattan, not Hancock. No one wears pink to dances here."

I fingered the dress. It wasn't that I didn't WANT to wear it. Low-cut, with spaghetti straps, it was nothing but two pieces of clingy black fabric, sewn together on the bias. Hanging around the hem were dozens of shiny black beads that made a clicking sound every time they moved.

It was gorgeous.

It was also so not me.

"Just put it on," Tory said.

I knew if I put it on, I'd never be able to let it go.

"No," I said. "I really shouldn't. YOU wear it to the dance, Tory. You would look fantastic in it."

"I already have a dress I look fantastic in," Tory said. "Just try it on. It can't hurt to try it on."

Embrace that which you fear.

She was right. It couldn't hurt to try it on.

So I did.

And just as I suspected, I knew I had to have it. It fit me perfectly, like a glove, showing off my arms and most of my back, and way more of my chest than I'd ever shown off before, outside of a swimming pool.

But it made me look . . . it made me look . . .

"NOT like a preacher's daughter," Tory said. "When Zach sees you in that, no way is he gonna want to be 'just friends' with you anymore."

And with that, I knew I was keeping it. Not that I said anything to Tory to make her think I agreed with her. Because I didn't. Zach was never going to think of me as more than just a friend. . . .

But it couldn't hurt to look a little sexy for a change. Mom was just going to have to deal. Or maybe I could talk Aunt Evelyn into saying her camera was broken. . . .

The morning of the dance, Tory's mom surprised us— Tory, Chanelle, and me—with an all-expense paid trip to her favorite spa in Soho. A manicure, pedicure, and our hair and makeup done by real professionals. Aunt

Evelyn said she did it because, "You girls are getting along so well. And, Tory, you've made so much progress this week."

There were actual tears in Aunt Evelyn's eyes as she said this at the breakfast table. It was so sweet, I practically got tears in my own eyes . . . just not for the same reason as Aunt Evelyn.

The truth was, for the first time in my life, things were going really well. I don't know if Lisa had done something to turn my luck around, or if, by some miracle, I'd done it myself. All I knew was that not only was I getting along great with Tory, but I also had a good friend—Chanelle, who'd graciously agreed to let Tory back into her social circle, so long as she continued to abstain from discussing toadstool collection from headstones at the lunch table—and even, if not a boyfriend, then at least a guy friend.

It was Zach, in fact, who'd shown me the flyer he'd found in the school's administrative office, announcing a scholarship—full tuition—for the next school year to any student with a high enough GPA who could show financial need.

The catch? The student also had to show that he or she could play an instrument. You had to audition, and everything.

"It's perfect for you," Zach said. "You've got it in the bag."

I didn't know about that. But I did know how much I had come to love New York. Not the Chapman School, so much, which I still thought was filled with mostly preppy snobs—quite a few of whom still blamed me for Shawn's expulsion . . . not that it bothered me so much anymore. I knew the truth and, more importantly, so did the people I actually cared about.

But I loved living with the Gardiners—now that Tory was being so nice to me at last—and I loved, loved, loved the city. I loved the busy streets and the gorgeous shop windows and the tall buildings and the Met and Carnegie Hall and the gyoza from Sushi by Gari and the bagels from H&H and the lox from Citarella. I had even gotten over my subway jitters, and could (almost) take the Number 6 train without the slightest hint of a knot in my stomach.

I was still hopeless at figuring out any of the other trains. But I had the 6 down pat.

And okay, I missed Stacy and my family.

But Hancock? I didn't miss Hancock a bit.

Especially not certain aspects of it.

And if I got the scholarship, I wouldn't have to go back. I knew Aunt Evelyn and Uncle Ted would let me stay with them. Sure, my parents would be sad (though Courtney wouldn't—one less person to hog the bathroom from her).

But even my mom and dad would understand that graduating from the Chapman School was going to look better on my admission application to Juilliard than Hancock High—because why shouldn't I try to get into Juilliard, with the way my luck was beginning to turn around? There were so many advantages to staying in the city over returning to Hancock . . . and I wasn't even counting the fact that Zach would be at Chapman—for one more year, anyway—too.

At six fifty-nine on the night of the dance—after having spent the day being pampered and styled to within an inch of my life (although the hairstylist, Jake, had taken one look at my hair and said, "No. Nuh-uh. We're not doing a thing to it. Maybe put a little bit of it up in the front with a clip—oh, yes, that's great—but no one is going near this girl with a flat iron. Do you hear me, people?")—I was fastening the jeweled strap to my evening sandal when the doorbell rang.

Then I heard Teddy—always the first to reach the door—cry, "Zach!"

"He's here, he's here," Alice came running into my room to announce.

She skidded to a halt on the threshold, though, and stared at me, openmouthed.

"Oh my gosh," she said. "Jean, you look like a princess!"

"Really?" I tugged nervously on my dress, staring at my reflection in the full-length mirror on my bathroom door. Suddenly, it all seemed too much—the dress was too tight, the neckline too low, my makeup too heavy, my heels too high, the pentacle around my wrist . . . yes, I was still wearing it, for luck, because if I ever needed luck, it was RIGHT NOW. But I thought wearing it on my wrist might be a little more discreet, since it was normally hidden beneath my shirt collars . . . especially since my neckline was *so* low, making the pentacle *so* noticeable when it was around my neck.

"Oh, Jean." Petra joined Alice in the doorway. "She's right. You look beautiful."

"The dress isn't too tight?" I asked anxiously.

"Not at all," Petra said. "Oh, I hope Mrs. Gardiner finds her camera!"

I said a silent prayer that Aunt Evelyn *wouldn't* find it . . . especially since I'd hidden it in the dryer.

"Well," I said. "Here goes nothing."

And I left my room and started down the stairs to the foyer.

Zach was there, looking impossibly handsome in his tuxedo, chatting with Uncle Ted. One hand was in his trouser pocket, while the other held a clear plastic box with a flower in it. He looked up the stairs when he heard Alice—who was trailing sneakily after me—let out a giggle.

And all of my nervousness about my looks disappeared. That's because whatever Zach had been saying to my uncle Ted, he no longer seemed to remember, as his voice trailed off and his gaze, seemingly locked on me, followed me down the stairs. When I finally got to the bottom of the staircase, Zach still didn't move. At least, not until Teddy, still hanging on to the front doorknob, cried, "Wow, Jean! You look great!"

Then Zach seemed to rouse himself. He said, "Yeah. Yeah, you look really . . . really—"

I stood there, my stomach suddenly in knots—what was he going to say? Surely not that I looked gorgeous or anything. That's not the kind of thing friends say to each other. . . .

"You look beautiful!" It was Aunt Evelyn who finished the sentence for him, holding her arms out to hug me. And Zach—I couldn't help but notice—didn't look in that big a hurry to correct her. "Oh, Jean, I wish I knew where I'd left the camera. Your mother's going to kill me!"

"That's okay, Aunt Evelyn," I said, rolling my eyes at Zach over Aunt Evelyn's shoulder as she hugged me. He finally managed a grin at me. "I'm sure she'll get over it."

"But *I* won't." She let go of me, then looked at Zach and me with tears in her eyes. "Oh, you two just look so . . . so . . ."

"Mom," Tory said, in a warning voice from the landing. "Don't you start crying. Then I'll start crying, and you'll make me ruin my makeup."

We all stared up as Tory, a vision in white (*but hadn't she said everyone wore black to the spring formal?*), descended the staircase. Her dress was, by Tory standards, almost modest, a froth of snow-white tulle with a satin bodice she'd paired with over-the-elbow gloves. If anyone looked like a princess, it was Tory. In comparison, as a matter of fact, I thought I looked . . . well, a little slutty.

"Tory!" her mother cried. "You look breathtaking! Oh, where did I put that camera?"

"Here, use mine, Mom," Tory said, drawing from her somewhat voluminous—for an evening bag—purse a small digital camera.

Great. After all the trouble I'd gone to, Mom was going to get a photo anyway. And of me looking the way Tory normally did, and Tory looking like . . . well, me. If I hadn't lost my head over the dress she'd gotten me.

She HAD said everyone wore black. So what was she doing in white?

We endured a round of photos, and then the humiliating production of Zach pinning on the corsage he'd gotten for me—a single, blood-red rose—which required MORE photos. (And this was particularly embarrassing since there wasn't a lot of dress to pin it to, just a strap. Aunt Evelyn had to step in and help—which was good, since I'd been feeling as if I were about to die, with Zach standing so close to me that I could see the tiny patch where he'd forgotten to shave just below his ear . . . which was definitely too close for comfort for me.)

Finally, at nearly seven thirty, they let us leave, and we climbed into the waiting limo and breathed a group sigh of relief.

"Shoot me," Tory said, from the middle of the fluffy white puddle her skirt made against the dark leather seat, "if I ever get like that, will you?" Meaning like her parents.

"I thought it was sweet," I said. "Mortifying. But sweet."

I tried not to let it show how impressed I was to be

riding in a limo. I had never been in one, of course. I saw there was a real decanter of whiskey in the light-up side bar, and a flat-panel TV that dropped down from the ceiling on a hinge.

But I didn't mess around with the buttons or anything, in case it gave away the fact that this wasn't something I did every day. Ride in a limo, I mean.

And then we were there. Because the Chapman School has no gym, they had to have their annual Spring Formal in a hotel ballroom. The hotel they'd chosen for this year's dance was the Waldorf-Astoria. The Waldorf is a huge fancy hotel on Park Avenue. When our limo pulled up in front of it, a doorman in red-and-gold livery opened the limo's door for us. Tory was the first one out, followed by me, then Zach.

Tory didn't wait for us, though. As we climbed out of the limo, she was already heading in through the big gold revolving doors.

"Okay," Zach said. "Someone's eager to get to the punch."

"I know," I said uncomfortably. "I hope she doesn't throw a fit when she finds out it's not sugar-free."

Then, looking down at me as we climbed the red-carpeted stairs to the revolving door, Zach asked, "Hey, did I tell you how great you look in that dress?"

"No," I said, blushing to my hairline and hoping he wouldn't notice. "You didn't."

"Well, you look great in that dress."

"Thanks," I said. What was going on here? Zach was

194

almost . . . well, *flirting* with me. "You don't look so bad yourself."

"Well," Zach said, with a mock dramatic sigh. "I do what I can."

Then we were through the revolving door and inside the high-ceilinged, dramatic lobby.

"Oh my God, Jean!" Chanelle was suddenly at my side, dragging a very alert-looking Robert behind her. "You look so fabulous! That dress is GREAT. Oh, hi, Zach. So what's with Tory?" Chanelle asked, not waiting for a reply. "She blew past us like a white tornado. And did you get a load of that dress? Who does she think she is, anyway? Princess Freaking Diana?"

"Yeah," I said. "I thought you said everyone wears black to the Spring Formal."

"Everyone DOES," Chanelle said, indicating her own black cocktail gown, which probably cost a YEAR of my allowance.

Robert looked at Zach and said, "Dude. You got any weed on you?"

"No," Zach said. "And I don't think you're allowed to smoke in here."

"I know," Robert said. "I was just, you know. Asking. For later."

"You guys have got to see the ballroom," Chanelle said, leading us toward a set of double doors outside of which sat a calligraphied sign that read, THE CHAPMAN SCHOOL SPRING FORMAL. "It is set up so cheesy. I don't know what the dance committee was thinking. Like, wait until you—"

But Chanelle never got out what she found so cheesy about the way the dance committee had set up the ballroom at the Waldorf-Astoria for the Chapman School Spring Formal. Because at that moment, Tory came rushing up to us, a tall, blond guy in a tux at her side.

"Hi, everyone," she said, grinning ear to ear. "I want you to meet the new man in my life. I didn't tell you all before, because I wanted it to be a surprise. This is my date. Oh, actually, Jinx, I think you know him."

And, surprised, I looked up into her date's face.

And almost fainted dead away.

CHAPTER EIGHTEEN

I have a very special thank-you I've been saving up, just for Jinx.

That's what Tory had said. I'd been a fool not to see it coming. I'd been a fool to ever think she hadn't meant it.

"I can't believe it," I murmured into the paper bag. "I just can't believe it."

"Shhh," Chanelle said. "Just breathe."

"I can't believe she was lying," I lifted my face out of the paper bag to say. "The whole time. She hasn't changed. She said she had a very special thank-you for me . . . and she did."

"If you don't breathe into the bag," Chanelle said, "you won't stop hyperventilating."

I breathed into the bag.

This was horrible. It was worse than horrible. It was the worst thing that had ever happened to me in my whole life.

And, you know, considering the kind of luck I've had in my life, that is really saying something.

Seeing that I was breathing a bit more regularly, Chanelle—whose concern for me was consummate and heartfelt . . . she was, after all, the person who'd hustled me into the ladies' room in the first place—quit checking out her reflection in the gilt-framed mirror above the sinks and went, "Better now?"

I nodded into the bag.

"Okay," she said. "Then tell me. Who's the guy?"

I lowered the bag and was surprised to find that I could breathe quite normally again. God bless the little bathroom attendant lady, who'd had a paper bag on hand, and who now sat gazing at me with motherly concern in her little black-and-white uniform.

"His name's Dylan," I said. "He . . . he's a friend of mine from back home." I couldn't tell her the truth. I couldn't. It was too horrible.

Chanelle arched a single brow. "That's it? So what made you freak like that?"

"I just . . . I was surprised to see him here, is all," I said. My heart had stilled its frantic thumping, but I still felt agitated. *What was he doing here? How had he gotten here?*

But I knew the answer to both questions. I knew only too well.

I have a very special thank-you I've been saving up, just for Jinx.

And when she walked in a second later, looking as if

butter wouldn't melt in her mouth, it was all I could do not to run, screaming, from the Waldorf-Astoria ladies' room.

"Oh, Jinx, there you are." Tory stood there, gleaming in her incredible white dress. She looked concerned, the picture of cousinly devotion. "Everyone's so worried about you, the way you just ran off back there. Is everything all right?"

"She's fine," Chanelle said, giving my shoulder a pat. "Just had a little bit of a shock."

"I know I should have told you about Dylan," Tory said, smiling at the bathroom attendant, who had risen and was rearranging her collection of hairspray bottles, bobby pins, and tampons and stuff, pretending not to be eavesdropping on our conversation. "But I thought it would be a nice surprise. Considering that you two were so . . . close."

"Oh," I said, feeling like I might soon have another use for the paper bag, my stomach was heaving so hard. "It was a surprise, all right."

"A pleasant one, I hope," Tory said, her dazzling smile never leaving her perfectly made-up lips. "Dylan's really glad to see you. Why don't you come out now and say hi? He and Zach are getting along really well."

"I *bet* they are," I said. How could I have been so stupid? How could I have actually thought she'd changed? Zach had warned me and I hadn't listened, because I'd wanted so badly to be right about her.

When the truth was, I couldn't have been more wrong.

"Come on, sillies." Tory, inspecting her reflection, gave her updo a final pat and turned to leave. "Let's not leave the boys waiting."

Chanelle turned to me. "Are you really all right now, Jinx?"

"Oh," I said, climbing shakily to my feet. Maybe I could quietly get Security. Yeah, that was it. I could just tell Security that Dylan . . .

. . . that Dylan what? He hadn't done anything. He was an invited guest of one of the Chapman School's students. Even if Security did agree to remove him, Dylan would, rightfully, protest. He'd probably end up making a scene. And if he didn't, Tory certainly would. It would ruin the dance . . . not just for me, but for Zach, too. Having Dylan removed would just draw *more* attention to the problem. . . .

When the truth was, I didn't even know for sure there still *was* a problem. A lot of time had passed since I'd last seen him. Maybe he was over it. Maybe it would be fine. . . .

Yeah. And maybe it was me Zach was in love with, and not Petra. Right.

"I'm just fine," I said in response to Chanelle's question. Because there was nothing—absolutely nothing—else I could do.

"Great." Tory leveled another beauty-queen smile my way. "Let's go."

My stomach was so knotted, it felt as if someone

had kicked me in the gut, I followed Tory and Chanelle back into the hotel lobby. Just as Tory had said, Dylan and Zach were shooting the breeze outside the ballroom doors, while Robert stood there, looking as if he wished he were someplace else . . . probably the Gardiners' gazebo.

I didn't blame him. I wished I were there, too.

Zach, who'd obviously been watching the ladies' room door for me, brightened when he saw me up and around. Dylan, apparently noticing Zach's smile, turned to face me and brightened as well.

"There you are," Dylan said as we approached. "We were worried."

"Just a girl thing," Chanelle said chipperly. "It's all good now."

"That's good to hear," Dylan said. He was smiling down at me, those blue eyes I'd once been so convinced I loved filled with concern . . . and adoration. Okay. Well, maybe he wasn't quite back to normal yet. But that didn't mean . . . "Now we can say hello properly. It's been a long time, Jean. It's really good to see you."

Then he stooped down to kiss me.

Just a kiss hello. Just a friendly *Haven't seen you in a while* kiss.

But I still took an involuntary step backward to avoid it.

Yes, that's right. I recoiled. Recoiled from the kiss of a totally hot guy I'd once been in love with.

201

Or thought I'd been in love with, anyway.

"It's good to see you, too, Dylan," I said quickly, offering out my right hand to seize his. "How are you?"

"Uh," Dylan said, looking down at our clasped hands as I gave him a hearty shake. "I'm fine."

"Good," I said, too loudly. Other people, filing into the ballroom in their evening finery, looked at me curiously. Every single girl but Tory was wearing black. "That's good. Well." I dropped his hand and wrapped my fingers around Zach's arm. "We better get in there. Get the party started and all. See you later."

And I proceeded to drag Zach into the Waldorf-Astoria ballroom, a fake smile plastered onto my face as we stopped by the seating chart to see which table we'd been assigned to.

"Are you going to tell me what the hell is going on?" Zach asked me, an equally fake smile plastered to his own face. Only on him, it looked adorable.

"Nothing," I said through my smile. "Nothing at all. Everything's fine. Oh, look, Table Seven. And here it is, over by the window."

"Everything is *not* fine," Zach said, as he nodded at some other juniors he knew who'd walked by and said, *Hey, Rosen.* "I'm not an idiot. It's not exactly reassuring when a guy's date gets a glimpse of some other guy at a dance and starts to hyperventilate."

"Oh," I said, dropping the smile. "You noticed that?"

"Yeah," Zach said, his own smile vanishing as well. "I

noticed that. Who is he, Jean? What's going on?"

"He's just . . ." My shoulders slumped . . . which was dangerous, because if I didn't stand up straight, the spaghetti straps of my dress would fall down, and that was not a good thing, considering they were pretty much the only thing keeping my dress up. "He's just . . . *him*," I said miserably.

"Him who?" Zach asked, sounding frustrated.

"*Him*," I said meaningfully. "The guy. The guy I came here to get away from."

"Wait." Zach looked over his shoulder at Tory and Dylan, who were checking the seating chart to see where they were supposed to be. "Him? He's THAT guy? The one who was stalking you?"

"Shhhh," I said, as a girl at a nearby table looked up sharply, having heard the word *stalking*. "He wasn't—I told you. He wasn't exactly stalking me. Well, I mean, he was, but . . ."

"He's here, isn't he?" Zach demanded. "I would call that stalking you."

"He's here because Tory invited him here," I said.

"Why the *hell* would she do that?"

"To get back at me," I said.

We'd reached our assigned seats at Table Seven. There were six places, each beautifully set with about thirty pieces of silverware and eight or so plates. This was a lot fancier than our school dances back in Hancock, where we had dinner before the dance, not AT it, and generally at the local Applebee's. Then we'd gather in the gym with a DJ and some party streamers, not a full orchestra and chandeliers.

"Tory flew him all the way out here," Zach said, "to get back at you for . . . what, exactly? The witch thing? What you did with the pills? Shawn? Or . . . *me*?"

"You name it," I said. "It could be any of the above. Or all of the above. Or even something else entirely. Who knows, with Tory?" And we'd thought she was doing so much better.

Correction. Everyone but Zach had thought she was doing so much better.

"Well, what's the deal with this guy?" he wanted to know. "Is he dangerous? Should we get Security? Jean—do you want to go?"

"No," I said, sitting down in my assigned seat. "Oh, no, Zach. It's nothing like that. He just . . . he just really liked me, okay? And the feeling wasn't mutual. At least, it was once, but not anymore. But he . . . he wouldn't leave me alone. He kept calling the house at all hours, and . . . and showing up there, too. Like in the middle of the night. My dad finally had to tell him to leave me alone. But even then, he kept showing up everywhere I was—church. The library. Babysitting jobs. He just kept sort of . . . following me. So finally we decided I should go away for a while. So I came here."

I couldn't, of course, tell Zach the whole truth. Not by a long shot. That at first I'd been thrilled by Dylan's attentions. I mean, I'd had a crush on him since freshman year, when he'd cut such a romantic and seemingly unattainable figure, captain of the football team, class president, straight-A student, sought-after by cheerleaders and lowly orchestra geeks such as myself.

When, in his senior year, he'd finally noticed me, then asked me out, I'd been over the moon. My girlfriends could hardly believe it, and neither could I—that I, Jinx Honeychurch, who, if it weren't for bad luck, would have no luck at all, had been asked out by Dylan Peterson, the most popular guy at Hancock High.

But it was true. It happened. And no sooner had we shared our first Blizzard at Dairy Queen together, than Dylan asked me to be his girlfriend, and I, thinking I'd died and gone to heaven, said I would.

But being Dylan's girlfriend, it turned out, was a lot more complicated than I'd ever anticipated. He expected me to be there for every single one of his games . . . even the ones that conflicted with my orchestra concerts. If I wasn't there, he got upset and said I didn't really love him. Which wasn't true.

At least at first.

Then he didn't just want me at his football games. He wanted me to be with him all the time. He wanted to drive me to school in the morning, then eat lunch with him, then watch him at football practice after school, then have dinner at his house, and do my homework with him . . . he'd have expected me to spend the night, I'm sure, if his parents—and mine—would have allowed it. He got upset if I said I wanted to go to the movies with my girlfriends, or stay home and practice my violin.

All too soon what I'd thought had been a dream come true turned into a living nightmare. . . .

Until I finally realized that whatever love I'd felt for him had disappeared, and I didn't want to spend ANY time with him, let alone every waking moment of the day, the way he wanted me to.

So I broke up with him.

I tried to be nice about it. I told him it wasn't him, it was me. I told him I wasn't mature enough for a relationship of this kind of intensity, and that things were going too fast for me. I said I needed some space, and that I had to concentrate on school and my music right now. I told him I needed to be able to see my friends and babysit on the weekends, not just spend all my time with him.

He said he totally understood and if I'd just give him another chance, he would let me have my space.

But the thing is, I didn't *want* to give him another chance. Because by then, I didn't even like him anymore.

So I told him a lie. I told him my parents had said I couldn't go out with him anymore, because he was too old for me, and they thought things were moving too fast. Hey, I'm a preacher's daughter, so what did he expect?

It was the wrong thing to say. I should have just said from the beginning, "I don't love you anymore."

Because then he decided that we were these star-crossed lovers, like Romeo and Juliet, and that my parents were out to keep us apart, and that if it weren't for them, we'd be together. That's when the phone calls and the showing up at the house in the middle of the night and the following me everywhere started.

I did finally tell him one night—after he'd woken me up at four in the morning by throwing pebbles at my window and begging me to come down to talk to him— that I didn't love him, and that he should just leave me alone.

But by that time, he was too far gone to believe me.

So I snuck out of town. I didn't know what else to do. I didn't want it turning into some kind of *Endless Love* scenario, where the guy tried to burn my house down or something (and, given my luck, that was exactly what was going to happen).

Why I couldn't manage simply to fall in love with a guy and have him love me back in a nice, healthy, normal way was just another indication of how badly the stars were aligned the night I showed up on Planet Earth. I mean, having to flee to the other side of the country to get away from an obsessive boyfriend might be Lindsey's idea of romance.

But it sure wasn't mine.

And now I had the pleasure of knowing that I hadn't even managed to do THAT successfully (flee to the other side of the country, I mean). Because here he was, at my new school's spring formal.

Nice. Very nice.

Why couldn't Tory have just shot me and gotten it over with? It would have been a heck of a lot less painful. And embarrassing.

"So all this time, when we thought she was doing so well," Zach said, taking his seat beside me at Table Seven, "Tory was planning this."

"I guess," I said. "And you don't have to say 'we.' You were right. Oh, Zach. I'm so sorry."

"*You're* sorry?" Zach shook out his napkin and laid it across his lap. "What have you got to be sorry for? It's not your fault."

"It is," I said, my stomach feeling worse than ever. "Believe me. It is."

"What, that some guy's crazy for you? Or that your cousin's got it in for you for some reason? Trust me, Jean. Neither is your fault."

But he didn't know the whole story. Not then, anyway.

"So what do you want to do, Jean?" he asked me. "Because I'm thinking it might be best if we just leave."

"Oh!" I said. "No, Zach. Not on my account. Or his, I guess. It'll be all right. Really."

It *had* to be. It couldn't possibly get any worse.

"Oh, hey!" Chanelle showed up at the side of the table, holding a little ivory card she'd picked up from the seating chart. "Table Seven?"

"Table Seven," Zach said, indicating the centerpiece, from which a number 7 stuck out. "Welcome."

"Goody," Chanelle said. "I'm so glad we're not stuck

with a bunch of dweebs. Sit down, Robert." Robert sat down next to Chanelle, who'd taken the empty seat across from Zach. "Look at all this silverware. What do we need all this stuff for? Oh my God, a fish fork? I hate fish. Who decided to have fish at a dance? Everyone's breath is going to reek."

And then, suddenly, just when I'd started to think I might be right, and things couldn't get worse, they did.

"Hi, everybody."

I heard the voice, but I didn't look up. I didn't have to.

"Isn't this fun?" Tory took the seat beside Zach. I felt the chair beside mine move, and knew Dylan had taken it. "Everything looks so pretty. The dance committee really went all out, huh?"

"They're serving *fish*," Chanelle said disdainfully, holding up her fish fork.

"I'm sure it will be delicious," Tory said, lifting her napkin and snapping it open expertly, before spreading it across her snowy white lap. "I can't wait."

"Neither can I," Dylan said. "This sure beats the Hancock Prom, doesn't it, Jinx?"

The sound of his voice, which had at one time thrilled my every nerve, now made me feel as if something were crawling up my back. That's how much I didn't love him anymore. I wondered if I had *ever* loved him, if I could feel this way about him now.

"Yeah," I said, in a voice completely lacking enthusiasm.

I couldn't believe it. This wasn't supposed to have happened. I was wearing my pentacle! And in my evening clutch, I had a little bag of spices—like the one the nice lady from Enchantments had made me for Zach. Wasn't that supposed to protect me from stuff like this? And what about that binding spell I'd done on Tory? She wasn't supposed to be able to hurt me.

Then I realized all of those things—the pentacle, the charm, and the binding spell—could only protect me from magic. What Tory had done tonight wasn't magic.

There was nothing magic about it at all. All it had taken was a little investigative skill and a major credit card.

"I'd like to propose a toast," Dylan said, lifting his water glass as soon as the waiter had come around and filled all of ours from a crystal pitcher.

I was positive I was going to throw up.

"To old friends," Dylan said, looking directly at me.

"To old friends," Chanelle echoed. "Aw, that's sweet. And to new ones, too, right, Jean?"

I lifted my water glass. "Yes." I was amazed I managed to get the word out.

I glanced in Zach's direction and saw he was looking at me. He lifted an eyebrow. His expression clearly read, *Come on. This isn't* so *bad.*

And he was right. It wasn't.

And then it was.

"So, Tory," Chanelle said, as a team of waiters placed our first course in front of us . . . a mesclun salad with a vinaigrette dressing. "How do you know Dylan?"

"Oh, it's a funny story, actually," Tory said, after swallowing a bite of her salad. "I knew Jinx had gone out with a guy named Dylan, but I didn't know his last name, or anything. So I called her sister Courtney, who was only too happy to tell me all about him."

That was it. When I got back to Hancock, the first thing I was going to have to do was kill Courtney.

If I lived through tonight, that is.

"So I gave Dylan a call, and we chatted"—Tory paused to flick a brilliant smile at Dylan . . . who, somewhat to my surprise, smiled right back at her, almost as if . . . well, almost as if he liked her—"and I thought what a fun surprise it would be for Jinx—who, though I know she probably hasn't mentioned it to all of you, has been pretty homesick—to fly him out here for the dance. So I did. Unfortunately, his plane was late, or he'd have met us at the house. But I think this worked out even better. Don't you, Jinx?"

"Oh, yeah," I said, moving the bits of mesclun around on the plate in front of me. No way could I bring myself to eat. "This worked out great."

"I thought it was the least I could do," Tory went on, in the same conversational tone. "Flying Dylan out here, and all. To show Jinx how grateful I am for all the things she's done for me since she got here. Like stealing my best friend. Oh, and narcing on Shawn. Oh, and snatching Zach out from under my nose."

Chanelle dropped her fork. Everyone else at the table—including Dylan—was staring at Tory in shock.

Robert was the first one to break the silence.

"You said you didn't narc on Shawn," he said, looking at me accusingly.

My eyes had filled with tears. I had thought this was as bad as it could get. Little did I know it would soon get much, much worse.

"I didn't narc on him," I said. Then, like a bolt from the blue, it hit me. "But I have a pretty good idea who did," I added, narrowing my eyes at Tory.

"Oh, right, Jinx," Tory said, with a laugh. "Like I'd narc on my own boyfriend—"

"Your own boyfriend who'd already put a down payment on a limo for tonight," I said. "And who might not take it too kindly if you ended up coming to the dance with someone else."

Robert's accusing gaze now swung toward Tory.

"You narced on Shawn so you could come here tonight with this Dylan guy?" he cried.

Tory, however, never took her eyes off me.

"You," she said, "are so going to wish you'd never been born."

"All right," Zach said, putting his napkin on the table, and standing up. "That's it. Jean, we're leaving. Now."

"Oh my God," Tory said, with a laugh. But she was still looking at me, not Zach. "You've even got *him* eating out of your hand now. It wasn't enough you had to steal my best friend and my own parents. You even had to go and steal the guy I love."

I felt myself turning as red as the carpet. Tory hadn't exactly spoken in the world's quietest voice, either. Everyone—at least, all of the people seated nearby—was staring at Table Seven now.

"Jean didn't steal anyone from you, Tory," Zach leaned down toward her chair to say in a low, steady voice. "Why don't you and I take a walk outside, all right? I think you need a little fresh air."

"Look at him," Tory said to me, with a sneer in Zach's direction. "So ready to do anything for you. Just like Dylan here. You should have heard how excited he was when I called and told him where you were. He could barely contain himself. I don't suppose either of these two ever bothered to consider *why* they might be so besotted with you."

The shiver that passed down my spine at that moment was ten times as strong as the one I'd felt when Dylan had spoken to me. Then, I'd just felt disgusted. Now, I felt as if someone had just walked over my grave.

Because I knew what Tory was about to do. I knew it as surely as I knew she'd been the one who'd turned in Shawn.

"Tory," I said, in a voice that sounded nothing like my own, it was so thin with fear. "Don't."

But it was too late. It was much too late.

Because Tory was already drawing her purse and reaching into it. I'd thought it was much too big for an evening accessory.

A second later, she had tossed a doll onto the middle of the table. A doll I recognized only too well. And I'm sure everyone else at Table Seven recognized it, too.

Since it looked exactly like Dylan.

CHAPTER NINETEEN

The doll had Dylan's eyes.

It had Dylan's build—the broad shoulders, the long legs.

It even had on Dylan's football uniform, in Hancock High's school colors of green and white. Dylan's number—number 12—was emblazoned on the doll's chest. Though perhaps Dylan and I were the only ones at the table who knew that. Except for Tory, who had obviously guessed.

The doll even had Dylan's hair. His REAL hair; hair that I had gone to a great deal of trouble to get way back when I had first set out to make Dylan fall in love with me. I had had to tell him we were taking hair samples from all the members of the football team to stitch onto a good luck pep quilt.

A pep quilt, for God's sake.

And then I'd had to go ahead and actually make a pep quilt, on account of not wanting Dylan to find out it was just HIS hair that I'd wanted.

Of course, if I'd known the spell was going to work as well as it had—a little TOO well, actually—I wouldn't have bothered making the quilt. Because no sooner had I finished the last stitch on the doll's face when the phone rang, and it was Dylan asking me out for that first, historic Blizzard.

I knew all that, of course. And, I had a feeling, so did Tory. Or most of it, anyway.

But no one else at Table Seven knew. Particularly not Zach. There was still a chance. There was still a—

"Did you ever wonder, Dylan," Tory asked in a sweet voice, "why it was that you fell so hard, and so fast, for a girl you didn't even have a single thing in common with?"

Dylan hadn't taken his gaze off the doll. He went, "Number twelve. That's my jersey number. What IS that thing? Is that supposed to be me? Is that my HAIR?"

"Yes," Tory said. "Yes, Dylan. That's the doll Jinx made of you, to make you fall in love with her. You see, originally she sewed some of *her* hair onto its head as well, so you wouldn't be able to get her out of *your* head. And it worked. Didn't it?"

Dylan looked from the doll, to Tory, to me, and back again.

"What *is* this?" he wanted to know. "Some kind of voodoo thing?"

"No, Dylan," I said. I could feel my world—which, let's face it, hadn't been a particularly great one, but it was the only world I had—slipping away from me. "It was just a game. I found this spell book at school, see, and . . . well, our grandmother always told us—"

"—that one of the daughters in our generation would turn out to be a great witch," Tory finished for me, for the benefit of the table. "One guess as to who that witch turned out to be."

Every eye at Table Seven was upon me. Not just Table Seven, either, but Tables Six and Eight were watching me pretty intently, too.

"It was just a game," I said, with a nervous laugh. "A silly game. I mean, no sane person could believe that you can make someone fall in love with you just by making a DOLL that looks like them."

"Yeah," Tory said. "Except that in your case, it worked, didn't it, Jinx?"

I shook my head, hard. "Come on," I said. "Let's be reasonable. That kind of thing just doesn't happen. It was just a coincidence, Dylan. I mean, that I made that doll, and you happened to ask me out. I mean, probably the only reason you noticed me in the first place was because I made up that story about needing your hair for that dumb quilt—"

Dylan looked perplexed. "You made up the story about the quilt? The pep quilt? But I saw it. All the guys donated their hair, too. . . ."

"I guess I could believe it was a coincidence," Tory said thoughtfully, "if it had only happened once."

I tore my gaze from Dylan's and stared at Tory's hand,

which was dipping, once more, into her bag.

Oh, no. Oh, for the love of God, no—

"But then you did it again," Tory said. "Didn't you, Jinx?"

And she threw the Zach doll down onto the table beside the Dylan doll.

I should have known that if she'd found one, she'd find the other. The first one—the Dylan doll—I'd hidden in what I thought was a brilliant location the very first night of my arrival in New York. I had brought the doll with me because I hadn't wanted one of my little sisters to find it in our room. And I hadn't thrown it away for the same reason I'd fished Tory's doll from the trash . . . I couldn't let it molder in some landfill. This was a doll of someone I'd once loved.

So I'd put the Dylan doll where I thought no one would ever think to look. And I'd put the Zach doll in the same place, a few weeks later.

Too bad I hadn't realized Tory had been spying on me the whole time. Or did she, too, like to hide things up the flue of that non-working fireplace in my bedroom?

Zach, staring down at what Tory had just thrown onto the table, asked, in a voice that sounded extremely distant, "Is that supposed to be me?"

"Zach," I said, feeling as if I were choking. "I did NOT make that one. I swear to God. I made the one of Dylan. But that was a long time ago, and I realized right away it was a horrible mistake—"

"Wait." Chanelle lifted her gaze from the two dolls to

218

my face. "Then you ARE a witch?"

I swallowed. How could this be happening? I mean, I realize it's me, and this sort of thing is bound to happen to someone like me.

But not anything THIS bad. My bad luck had never been quite THIS awful before.

"I cast a spell," I admitted. What else could I do? *Embrace that which you fear.*

That's what Lisa had said. And I certainly feared admitting to anyone what I'd done. Maybe, if I came clean now, things would get better. "I thought I was doing white magic. I didn't realize that white magic is NOT about trying to force people to do anything against their will, or manipulate their emotions. I didn't know that when I made that doll of you, Dylan, and I'm really sorry. As soon as I realized, I tried to undo the spell by taking my hair off it. But . . . but I guess it didn't work."

Robert, across the table, looked from the dolls to me and went, "Dude. This is freaking me out. Is she a witch, or what?"

"She's a witch," Tory said firmly. "I just thought all of you should know. First she made poor Dylan fall head over heels in love with her. And then I guess she decided having one guy completely bananas for her wasn't enough, so she came to New York and immediately set her sights on poor Zach here—"

"I didn't make the Zach doll!" I shouted, standing up. "Tory did! She showed it to me the first night I got to New York. She thinks SHE's the witch Grandma was always talking about, and she made this doll and tried to get me to join her coven. And then when I said I wanted nothing to do with it—because I'd learned, the hard way, what happens when you mess around with magic—she got mad."

Breathing hard, I looked around the table at the stunned faces of Dylan and my friends. None of them looked as if they believed me. Zach couldn't even look me in the eye.

"Zach," I said, appealing to him. Because it was his opinion, out of everyone's, I cared about most. "You've got to believe me. I mean, just look at this doll." I picked up the Zach doll. "It looks nothing like the doll I made. I mean, a . . . a . . . monkey could sew a better doll than this."

"I think," Tory said quietly, when Zach didn't respond right away, "that you had better go, Jinx. No one wants you here."

I looked at her then. I mean, really looked at her.

And I realized just how brilliantly she'd managed to pull off this little scheme of hers, down to the smallest detail. In her white ballgown and virginal makeup, SHE actually looked like the preacher's daughter—the one who, naturally, would be telling the truth. Whereas I, in the slinky black dress she'd picked out for me and my wild red hair, looked every inch of what she was claiming I was . . . a practicing witch, who had set out to win the heart of not one, but two of the most popular boys in both schools I had attended that year.

I had to hand it to her. She had succeeded, and probably even beyond her own wildest dreams.

But she wasn't finished yet. The coup de grace was still to come.

"I really think," Tory lowered her voice to say, as if it were "just us girls" talking—though of course by now, the whole room was listening . . . even the waiters, who'd started coming around with the fish course—"that you might want to take a lesson from our great-great-great-great-grandmother Branwen, Jinx. Because, you know, she was burned at the stake for witchcraft. We wouldn't want that happening to you, now, would we?"

I couldn't believe she was repeating back to me what I'd told her about Branwen. I couldn't believe she'd even be willing to bring in the horrible way Branwen had died, just to make me look bad in front of Zach.

But I shouldn't have been surprised. I mean, if she was willing to lie about the doll, she'd stoop to anything.

"Fine," I said, in a voice that shook. "That's just fine, Tory. You won. Because you know what? I . . . I don't even care anymore."

And I got up and turned away.

And, in front of all those people, with all those stares boring into my back, I stalked from that ballroom, hoping against hope I'd have the strength to get out of there before I started crying.

I thought I heard a guy's voice call my name, but

whether it was Dylan or Zach, I couldn't tell.

All I knew was that, whoever it was, I couldn't face him. Not then. Not without bursting into tears.

I made it out of the revolving doors and onto Park Avenue. There, to my relief, the doorman asked, "Need a cab, miss?"

I nodded, and he flagged down a cab for me. I crawled into the backseat, grateful I'd thought to bring enough cash with me to get myself home, if I needed to . . . a lesson my preacher mother had drilled into me since childhood.

"Where to, miss?" the cabbie asked me.

I wanted to say the airport. I wanted to say Penn Station, or Grand Central, or any place that would get me on a plane or a train out of New York and back to Iowa.

Only I didn't have THAT much money on me.

So I just said, "Three twenty-six East Sixty-ninth Street, please."

And the cabbie nodded, and turned the meter on, and took me home.

I didn't cry until I got to my room. Fortunately, I didn't run into anyone in the hallway or on the stairs. Alice was already in bed, and Teddy was away at a sleepover, and Petra and Willem, babysitting while Aunt Evelyn and Uncle Ted were at one of the many parties they are constantly invited to, were in the den watching a movie. No one heard me come in.

And no one heard me weeping into my bathwater after I'd shed my finery and crawled into the big marble tub. I wept until my eyes were red and swollen, until I couldn't squeeze out another drop. I kept the water running the whole time, so if Petra did come up to check on Alice, she wouldn't hear me crying.

How could it have happened? I'd been humiliated in front of the entire school—made to look like a bigger freak than they already thought I was. I didn't care so much about what Robert or even Chanelle thought about me. But Zach! How could she have done it in front of Zach? I mean, I know she'd liked him. I know she was upset that my spell on Dylan had worked and hers on Zach hadn't.

But did she HAVE to do that in front of Zach?

And then, even as a fresh new wave of tears seemed to appear, they suddenly dried up.

Because a new thought had occurred to me, one I'd never considered before.

Was THAT what this was all about? Was it less about a boy, and more about the fact that MY spell had worked and hers hadn't? Was Tory really jealous because she knew *I* was the witch Branwen had promised would come along? Was she jealous because she thought it should be HER?

Because I'm not afraid to use her gift the way you are. That's what Tory had said to me.

It seemed so stupid. I mean, what did it even matter?

223

My powers, such as they were, had only brought me misfortune and heartache. Sure, I'd saved Zach from that bike messenger. But that hadn't been magic. I had merely been in the wrong place at the right time.

And the power going out the night I was born . . . that had just been a thunderstorm.

And Willem winning that trip to see Petra . . . that had just been a fluke. It had nothing to do with the binding spell I'd cast against Tory, or the protection spell I'd put on Petra.

And Dylan . . . poor Dylan. He had just felt like falling in love, and I had come along, with this enormous crush on him . . . of course he'd fallen in love with me.

None of this was proof I had the makings of a witch.

Except, I guess, to Tory, who'd probably bragged to her coven about her witch ancestry, and her destiny as the one true witch of our generation.

And then I'd had to come along and ruin it all for her.

It all made perfect sense. Really, it was no wonder she was so mad.

But if being the witch in the family meant so much to her, she could have it. I'd lift the binding spell, and—

What was I even TALKING about? THERE WAS NO SUCH THING AS MAGIC.

Because if there were, what had happened tonight would never, ever have happened. My necklace—that stupid pentacle necklace the lady from Enchantments had given me—would have protected me.

But it hadn't. It hadn't because the whole thing was a crock. There was no such thing as magic. Any more than there was such a thing as luck. At least such a thing as good luck. Because that was something that had never once come my way.

And I was so furious over the whole thing—so sick of it all—that I yanked off the pentacle and threw it across the bathroom. I tried not to look where it landed, either, so I couldn't go back later to pick it up. Let Marta find it and think it was trash.

I wished I could throw away my life as easily.

It must have been an hour later—I was already in bed, in my most hideous pajamas, the pink flannel ones with the butterflies on them—when there was a tap at my door.

"Jean?" It was Petra.

"Come in," I said. Petra was one of the few people I thought I could stand at that moment.

"I thought I heard you run a bath," she said, gazing at me concernedly from the doorway. "You came home early, didn't you?"

"Yeah," I said. "It wasn't that much fun, it turned out."

"Did you and Zach have a fight?" Petra asked kindly.

"You could say that," I said.

"I thought so. Because he is here."

I sat bolt upright in bed. "HERE? NOW?"

"Yes, he is downstairs. He would like to see you."

Ha. I bet he would. So he could tell me . . . what? That he thought we shouldn't see each other anymore? That he'd decided to go back to his policy of laissez-faire—and that one of the things he was adopting that attitude toward from now on was me?

Well, I wasn't going to give him the satisfaction. No way was I going down there. Not without any makeup on, with my hair looking all wild and frizzy from the steam the way it did. Not in my butterfly pajamas. That was no way to look during a breakup. Not that we were breaking up, because we'd never been going out. Anyway, he could break up with me or whatever—tomorrow, when I had some lip gloss on.

"Could you tell him I already went to sleep?" I asked her.

Petra knit her brow. "Of course I can, if you want me to. But are you sure that's what you want, Jean? He seems very worried about you. He said . . . he said something happened tonight. Something with Tory?"

"Yeah," I said. I'm sure he seemed worried. Probably because he was afraid of what kind of spell I was going to put on him, after he dumped me. That was all. "Yeah, I'm sure."

"Well," Petra said. "All right. Do you want to talk about it?"

Did I want to talk about it? I didn't even want to THINK about it, ever, ever again.

"You know what?" I said. "I really just want to go to sleep, if that's okay."

"That's fine," Petra said, with a nice smile. "Just remember, I'm here if you need me. You don't even need to be shy about Willem. If you need anything, just knock on the door downstairs. All right?"

"All right," I said, managing a smile. "Thanks. And good night."

"Good night, Jean," Petra said, and closed the door behind her.

Petra was so sweet. I was really going to miss her when I went home.

Which would be, I'd already decided, just as soon as I could arrange a ticket. Because I couldn't stay in New York a second longer. I certainly couldn't go back to school on Monday. I would face Zach tomorrow, because I owed him that much, anyway.

But I was going back to Hancock, where I belonged. After Tory, handling Dylan would be a snap.

Besides, maybe after finding out about the doll, he'd cool off a bit. Guys don't like knowing they've been lied to and manipulated. Zach was proof enough of that. Maybe Dylan would follow Zach's lead. At least ONE good thing would come out of all of this, then.

I'd told Petra to tell Zach I was asleep, and I'd turned out the light after she'd left, as if to make it so.

But sleep was a long time coming. I lay awake, going over the scene at Table Seven in my head, over and over.

But no matter how many times I tried, I couldn't think of a single thing I could have said to make Zach believe me. Tory really had done a *superb* job of manipulating the situation to her liking. I hoped, after this, that she got what she wanted. Zach. No more Petra. Branwen's magic powers. Whatever it was. Certainly, few people had ever worked as hard for it as she had.

At least, not in as screwed-up a way.

I don't know what time I fell asleep. But I do know what time it was when I woke up. Two in the morning.

I know because I opened my eyes and saw the red digital numerals on the clock by my bed.

The reason I'd woken up? Well, that was the funny thing.

It wasn't because I'd suddenly become filled with a sensation that—for once—everything was going to be all right. It wasn't because, despairing as I'd been when I'd fallen asleep, I'd woken with a sense of calmness, a sense that there was nothing—nothing in the world—that I needed to be afraid of, although both these things were true.

No, I woke because there was someone standing beside my bed, and whispering my name.

"Jean," the voice said. *"Jean."*

It was a girl, wearing a long white dress.

But it wasn't Tory, still dressed in her spring formal finery.

Because this girl was smiling at me—and not in a mean way, but as if she truly liked me. Plus, she had long red hair.

And even though I'd never met her before, I knew her name. I knew it as well as I knew my own.

"Branwen?" I said, sitting up.

CHAPTER TWENTY

But the minute I sat up, she was gone. The smiling red-haired girl in the long white dress had disappeared.

If she'd ever been there at all.

Because surely she had just been a dream. In a state between waking and sleeping, I'd only thought I'd seen my ancestress standing by my bed, saying my name. That had to have been it. Because I didn't believe in ghosts, any more than I believed in magic.

At least, not as of tonight, anyway.

It was as I was telling myself this that I felt something around my neck. Something that hadn't been there when I'd gone to sleep. Reaching up, I realized it was the pentacle necklace Lisa had given me.

The one I distinctly remembered taking off my wrist and throwing across the room earlier in the evening, not even looking to see where it had fallen.

And yet now it was around my neck.

A feeling of—what? Not fear. Because I wasn't frightened. And not dread, either. My stomach didn't hurt at all. But something, anyway, gripped me. I still felt the strange calm I'd experienced on waking, but now it was coupled with . . . happiness.

I was *happy*.

What was going on? Why wasn't I afraid? Necklaces don't just fasten themselves. Someone had found this necklace and put it back around my neck. But who? Who could have come into my room and done something like that, so quietly and gently that I hadn't woken up? Petra?

Or the ghost of my great-great-great-great-grandmother looking out for me when I most needed her? Showing me that—just as I had always suspected—I really was the daughter she'd meant—the one who was destined for greatness as a witch. Not Tory.

Only me. It had always only been me.

I'd just needed to believe. In her.

In myself.

Suddenly, I knew sleep was gone. My skin was tingling as if I'd been electrified. I jumped out of bed and went to the window. A dim blue light was coming in through the gauzy curtain liners—I'd forgotten to draw the drapes themselves. I assumed the light was from the neighboring apartment buildings behind Tory's house.

But when I pushed the curtain liner aside, I saw that

the light came from a full moon, hanging heavy and white in the night sky, so bright that there was a slight rainbow around it.

A waning moon, I knew from my reading of the witch book I'd bought, was a time for doing banishment spells. A waxing moon was when, traditionally, witches did spells for prosperity and growth.

But on the night of a full moon . . . well, pretty much anything goes. Anything is possible under a full moon. That's why so many people end up in the emergency room on the nights when the moon is full.

At least, that's what they said on *ER*.

How odd that tonight, of all nights, there should be a full moon.

Or was that why Branwen had finally been able to appear before me? Because of the moon . . . and my need?

Then I heard something from down in the garden. It sounded, actually, like Mouche. But what would Mouche be doing outside at night? Alice always remembered to call for her and bring her inside after dark. The cat slept with her every night. Who could possibly have let Mouche out?

Then I noticed something strange. There was a light on in the gazebo.

No. Surely not. I had to be imagining things . . . the way I'd imagined seeing Branwen. If I *had* imagined seeing Branwen.

But no. There it was again. Not just a light, but many lights, almost as if . . .

. . . as if someone were lighting candles down there.

Someone who looked a lot like my cousin Tory.

And suddenly, I knew why Branwen had chosen that night, of all nights, to appear to me. I even knew why she'd found my necklace and fastened it back around my neck.

Because it was time. It was time to confront my cousin Tory.

Not turning on a light—I didn't want Tory to see it, know I was up, and have advance warning that I was coming to see her—I slipped out of my pajamas and into jeans and a sweater. I carried a pair of loafers in my hand as I left my room and made my way down the stairs, so my footsteps wouldn't wake anyone. When I got to the door leading to the garden, I stepped into my shoes and started down the stairs to the garden.

There was plenty of light—bluish, but still a lot of it— to see by.

But I didn't need the light of the moon to see the yellow glow coming from behind the frosted glass panes of the gazebo. Or the three slender shadows cast by it.

It was Tory. Tory and her coven.

And suddenly I remembered the mushrooms. The mushrooms Tory had asked Chanelle to help her scrape off a tombstone by the light of a waxing moon. The moon was at its fullest now. It would begin waning tomorrow. Whatever she was intending to use them for, it had to be happening tonight.

And whatever she was intending to use them for, it had to be something bad, if I knew Tory. It couldn't be anything to do with me. She had decimated me at the dance. She had to know that. No, whoever this spell was destined for—Petra, Zach, who knew?—it wasn't me. Tory knew she was well rid of me.

For the first time since waking that night, I felt something other than an eerie calm.

Anger. I felt angry.

Not at what Tory had done to me—I'd deserved that, for what I'd done to Dylan. No, I was angry that, having witnessed the direct results of my own attempt to manipulate the will of others tonight, Tory still couldn't see that doing so was wrong.

Well, enough was enough. It was over. She had to be stopped. *I* was going to stop her.

Which is when I flung open the glass door to the gazebo to tell her . . .

. . . until what I saw inside caused my voice to dry up in my throat.

There they were, all three of them, Tory still in her virginal white dress from the dance. Gretchen and Lindsey, on the other hand, were all done up in their usual heavy black eyeliner and were wearing all black. They were sitting around what looked like a small altar on the glass-topped table in the middle of the gazebo, complete with dozens of lit candles (black ones, of course) and an empty chalicelike thing in the middle of the table/altar.

And they didn't look at all surprised to see me. Well, Tory didn't, anyway.

"There," she said, with a certain amount of satisfaction in her voice. "I told you she'd come, ladies. Didn't I?"

Lindsey's only response—not surprisingly—was to giggle. But Gretchen, throwing me a scathing look, said, "I don't get it, Tor. How'd you know?"

"Because she's weak," Tory said. That's when I saw what she was holding in her hands, beneath the glass-topped table. It was Mouche, struggling to get free and making quite a ruckus about it.

The same ruckus I'd heard from my room.

Which was why Tory abruptly let the cat go. Because Mouche had done what Tory had needed her to.

She'd lured me down to the gazebo. Exactly where Tory had wanted me.

"If she's weak," Gretchen said darkly, "then what do we want her for?"

"I told you. It's not her we want," Tory said. "It's her blood."

Which is when it finally dawned on me what was going on—why they were sitting around the empty chalice.

And what I was there for.

Like the blood from my face, I felt all of the Branwen-instilled resolve drain away. I whirled around to leave—but I wasn't quick enough. I got the door open—just enough for Mouche to run out—but Gretchen, who turned out to be as strong as she was tall, grabbed me and pulled me back, shoving me roughly into the wrought-iron chair across the table from Tory's.

"Bind her hands," Tory commanded.

And Lindsey and Gretchen dutifully produced a black satin cord—probably the sash to one of their father's bathrobes—and began to wind it—not very loosely, I don't mind saying—around my wrists. In fact, they tied me up quite tightly.

"You guys," I said. I told myself not to panic. It was probably only some kind of stupid hazing ritual. Probably, they were going to make me join their dumb coven and pledge some stupid oath. Just a little bloodletting, to make us "soul sisters," or whatever. Still. "I think you cut off the circulation to my fingers."

"Shut up," Tory said.

"Okay," I said. "But if my fingers turn black and start falling off—"

"I said, SHUT UP."

That was when Tory got up from her chair and hit me. Hard. Open-palmed, across the face.

I guess you could say it was more of a slap than a hit. Still, it hurt. For a minute, I saw stars.

That's when I realized this probably wasn't about hazing after all.

"Is everything ready?" Tory asked her two accomplices, who nodded. Gretchen had a look of excitement on her face. Only Lindsey seemed a bit taken aback by the slap. At least, from what I could observe, through eyes that had automatically filled up with tears at the blow. Tory was much stronger, physically, than I'd ever given her credit for. That slap had HURT.

"All right," Tory said. She returned to her seat.

"Tonight, under this new moon, a time for new beginnings, I am going to right a wrong," she began. "A hundred and fifty years ago, one of the most powerful witches of all time, Branwen, who was born with the gift of magic, predicted that a descendant of hers would inherit her great powers. By every law that is natural and right, that descendant should have been me. But for some completely screwed-up reason, it looks as if it's my cousin Jinx."

"It's not," I said. Because, though I had seen Branwen in my own room that very night, I suspected that, based on her own experiences, she'd probably agree that denying possession of any witchlike abilities was the way to go. "It's not me."

Tory glared at me. "Don't," she said, "interrupt the ceremony."

"But it's not me, Tory," I said desperately. "Come on, this is stupid. How could I have magic powers? You know I'm the unluckiest person on the face of the planet—"

"How do you explain Dylan, then, and his devotion to you?" Tory snapped.

"That was just a fluke."

"Shawn?"

"That was *you*," I said. "*You're* the one who got him expelled."

"Sure," Tory said. "But everyone blames you. What about Zach?"

I blinked at her.

"Well, Jinx? What. About. Zach."

And, just like that, it was back. The anger I'd felt earlier. The anger that Lisa had told me I would need when the time came.

"I told you a million times," I said. "Zach doesn't like me that way. We're just friends . . . and we're probably not even *that* anymore, thanks to YOU and that stupid doll of YOURS, so—"

Tory stood up, one hand raised as if to hit me again. I glared at her, daring her—just daring her—to try it. If she came one step closer, I'd kick her in the face.

But Lindsey, of all people, stopped her by whining, "Can we just get this over with? I'm starving. And you know what happens when my blood sugar gets too low."

Tory glared at her.

"Fine," she said.

That's when Tory picked up the knife. A *huge* knife— a decorative one, like the kind you buy at those stores that sell ornamental knives, like those used in the *Lord of the Rings* movies.

One look at that knife, and I was done. That was it. I sprang up from the chair—only to have Gretchen shove me back and hold me down with both hands pressed, hard, to my shoulders, while I squirmed. Seeing I wasn't going to escape that way, I opened my mouth to scream—

But Tory, anticipating the move, shoved both her long,

silk gloves into my mouth, effectively gagging me.

"Stop struggling, Jinx," Tory was saying, in what was actually quite a soothing voice, for her. "This is what you want, remember? You've always wanted just to be normal, right? Well, as soon as we get enough of your blood for me to drink, I'll assume your powers, and you won't have to worry anymore. I've made a banishing potion from some very rare mushrooms. You can drink it down, and you won't have to worry about bad luck anymore. All the powers you inherited from Branwen will be gone. Instead, I'll have them."

Okay. This was bad. This was really bad. I'd had some bad luck before this, it was true . . . but this was definitely the worst. I had to get out of this.

But how? I was completely helpless. Gretchen was strong. That cord was tied so tightly. I couldn't cry out. What could I do?

What does *anyone* do when all hope is gone, and all else fails?

What was it that Lisa from Enchantments had said? Tory can't hurt me if I . . . if I . . . if I what? *Why couldn't I remember?*

Embrace the magic.

But how could I? How could I embrace something that had caused me nothing but grief for so long? I mean, look what had happened with Dylan. Look what had happened to the people in the hospital the night I was born. Look what had happened tonight at the dance. I couldn't embrace something that had messed up so many lives, something that I'd assumed was *bad*.

"Wait a minute," Lindsey said. "You're going to *drink* her blood?"

"What did you expect?" Tory demanded. "It's a blood ritual. Duh."

"I know," Lindsey said, growing, if such a thing were possible, even paler. "But I didn't know you were going to *drink* it. Do I have to, too?"

"Do you want me to be a real witch," Tory roared, "or don't you?"

"Well," Lindsey said. "Yeah. I guess. I don't know. But are you really going to make her drink that stuff with the mushrooms in it? What if she gets sick? They could be poisonous, for all you know."

"It won't matter," Tory said. "No one will believe her. They'll think she poisoned herself, on account of what happened at the dance. And by then I'll have her powers— which she never appreciated, much less learned how to use properly. And Mom and Dad'll be putty in my hands." To me, Tory said, in a voice that was soothing again, "And Zach will love me, not her. Just wait and see."

But I barely heard her. Because I was thinking, *What if what Lisa had said was true, and all of the awful things that had happened to me hadn't been caused by bad luck, but by fear . . . fear turned inward? Fear of what I really was.*

Fear of WHO I really was.

The magic will save me. Branwen will save me . . .

. . . if I embrace that which I fear.

240

And suddenly, my mind emptied. Instead, I thought about the magic and how it could save me. I thought about the moon, so bright and high, with that rainbow around it. I thought about the roses bursting into bloom all around the garden. I thought about Branwen, and how she'd given me back my necklace, and how calm I'd felt after I'd seen her, smiling, beside my bed.

And I thought about Zach, right next door. All he had to do was just look out his window. Then he'd see the gazebo . . . he'd see me.

"I don't know how much longer I can hold her." Gretchen's voice sounded shaky with fear. I hadn't noticed that before. But now, it was as if all my senses had been heightened. I was aware of the smell of roses in the air, so sweet.

Wake up, Zach. Look at the moon, Zach. I'm here, Zach. I'm down here.

"Fine." Tory looked furious. "Then just shut up and watch while I do my thing."

Tory then proceeded to "do her thing" by holding up the knife so that the blade glinted in the moonlight that sliced through the glass ceiling of the gazebo. Then Tory intoned, "In the name of Hecate, and Branwen, and . . . and all of the witches in creation, I draw from this woman that which rightfully belongs to me."

She signaled for Lindsey to reach down and grab my bound wrists—which she did, though I struggled to keep them from her, while at the same time struggling to break free from Gretchen's heavy grasp—and hold them out across the chalice.

And, without the slightest bit of hesitation, Tory started to bring down the shiny blade she held.

Which was when three things happened simultaneously. Lindsey let go of my hands and cried, "Oh my God, Tory! You can't *really*—"

And I raised my knee against the underside of the table as hard as I could, tipping the heavy glass—and the chalice, the candles, and mushroom potion on top of it—toward Tory.

And I heard the gazebo door crash open, and a familiar, masculine voice say, "What the *hell* is going on here?"

CHAPTER
TWENTY-ONE

"Zach!" Tory cried, scrambling to her feet. "Oh my God! What are you doing here? How nice of you to drop by!"

Zach, however, didn't seem to be in the mood for social niceties. Maybe it was the glass tabletop that had rolled over onto the hem of Tory's skirt, which she was trying desperately—yet casually—to pull free. Or maybe it was the knife she still held in one hand, or the mushroomy potion spilled all over her dress.

Maybe it was Gretchen's and Lindsey's guilt-stricken expressions.

Or maybe it was the fact that I was bound and gagged and sprawled in an ignominious heap on the gazebo floor.

In any case, he didn't respond to Tory's question. Instead, he knelt down beside me and pulled the gloves from my mouth.

"Are you all right?" he wanted to know.

I nodded. I don't think I could have spoken if I'd wanted to. Not because my cousin had just tried to kill me. But because Zach had rushed down to rescue me without remembering to put a shirt on.

Maybe Tory *had* killed me, and I had died and gone to heaven.

Except that if this was heaven, why was Lindsey crying?

"Oh, Zach, *please* don't tell Mr. and Mrs. Gardiner about this," she begged. "Mrs. Gardiner's on the same volunteer board at Sloan-Kettering as my mom. She'll KILL me if she found out I was playing around at being a witch."

That's when Tory shrieked, "LINDSEY! SHUT UP!" And then began to babble.

"We tried to stop her," Tory said. "Honest to God, Zach. But Jean was so upset, you know, over what happened— my outing her as a witch at the dance, and all—that she tried to kill herself. This is how we found her. We were just about to call nine-one-one—"

"She gagged *herself*?" Zach demanded harshly. "And tied her own hands together? Nice try, Tory. But I heard what you were saying to her, you sick—"

Then Zach said some very bad swear words. The kind my mother would have charged him a quarter for, if he'd said them back in Hancock.

"God," Tory said, sounding mad. "Fine. Don't believe us. The only reason you're on her side is because she cast a love spell on you. How does it feel, knowing you're just

244

a victim of her manipulative witch MAGIC?"

"No," I tried to say. "Don't listen to her. I did use magic. I called you here with magic, Zach. But to help me. Not to love me. Never to love me. That doll was hers! That doll was hers!"

But nothing came out of me except a croaking noise. I couldn't speak, because my throat was as dry as sand.

"The only victim I can see here is Jean," Zach was saying in a harsh voice. "What is *wrong* with you, Tory? You could have really hurt her."

"Oh, sure." Tory was sniffling now. "Take her side. That's very nice. I've known you since I was in kindergarten, but take the side of the person you've only known a month—"

But Zach wasn't listening. "Give me that knife," he said to Tory, who mutely handed it to him, while Gretchen said, actually sounding scared, "I never thought it would go this far, Zach. I never thought Tory really meant to hurt her. When she told us about it, she said she would just prick her a little. Also, that Jean wouldn't mind, that she was sick of her bad luck, or something, and wanted to get rid of it and give it to her."

I said, "Never! I will never surrender my power! I've embraced it! I don't fear it anymore!"

But all that came out was more croaking.

"Only that it wasn't bad luck"—Gretchen was the one babbling now—"that it was magic, and she—Jean— just didn't know how to use it properly. And that if Tory drank her blood—Jean's blood—that doll thingy of hers would work, and you'd love her the way she wanted you to—"

"GRETCHEN!" Tory yelled. "SHUT UP!"

Zach used Tory's knife to cut the cords that were keeping my hands tied. It was only when he pulled me to my feet that he noticed—we both noticed—I couldn't walk so well. Not from anything Tory had done, but from the pain in my knee, where I'd rammed it so hard into the glass-topped table in order to tip it over.

"Come on," Zach said, slipping an arm around my waist. "Lean on me."

And he helped me hobble from the gazebo and out into the fresh night air of the garden, where Mouche met us, with a tiny, inquisitive "Mrow?"

"We can't leave Mouche outside," I tried to say. "Alice will freak out if she's not on her bed when she wakes up."

But my voice was still too rusty from the gag, and all that came out was, "Mouche."

"I know," Zach said. "I'll come out and get her after I get you inside. Don't worry."

And then he was banging on a door, and a few seconds later, I heard Petra's voice say sleepily, "Yes? Who is—oh, Zach? What are you—"

Then in a much less sleepy voice, she said, "Jean!"

Then the moonlight disappeared, and we were in Petra's snug basement apartment, the door to which was right off the garden. Zach was lowering me onto Petra's couch, and I had time to notice that Willem wasn't sleeping there after all. He was standing in the doorway to Petra's bedroom wearing nothing but a pair of boxer shorts and a really confused expression. He looked incredibly cute.

Although not as cute as Zach, in nothing but the jeans he'd thrown on so hastily, they weren't even buttoned properly.

Zach's hands were all cut up, too. What had happened to Zach's hands?

Oh. The roses.

"Oh my God," Petra was saying. "What happened?"

The roses. He'd cut them on the roses, climbing over the wall.

But Petra wasn't talking about Zach, it turned out.

"She's all right. She just needs some water," Zach said. Then, three more words, uttered so coldly, they chilled my heart: "It was Tory."

"Her wrists—"

"They tied her up," Zach said shortly.

"Oh my God. I should wake the Gardiners," Petra said.

"NO!" a shrill voice called out.

And that's when I realized Tory had followed us from the gazebo.

"Petra, don't!" Tory cried. Her expression—Willem had turned on the overhead light—was one of wild-eyed, near hysteria. She stood there in her potion-smeared white ball gown, looking like Cinderella at the ball—after realizing the clock had struck midnight. "Don't tell Mom and Dad! Jinx told me she wanted to get rid of her powers. She told me she couldn't handle them . . . she was tired of always having such bad luck. I was trying to help her. Honest."

"Powers?" Willem asked. "What are these powers she speaks of?"

"Tory," Petra said, as she knelt beside me and offered me a glass full of water, which I took and immediately drained. "Not now."

"Wait," Tory said. She was crying now. I watched as tears streamed down her pretty face. "It was a game. That's all it was. Jinx was in on it. She liked it."

"Oh, is that right?" Zach's voice was hard. "And the dead rat? She liked that? And everyone in school thinking she's a narc, when it was you—don't deny it—who turned in Shawn . . . your own boyfriend? And what about the stunt you pulled tonight at the dance, bringing that guy from Iowa? I could see how much she liked that." Zach's voice dripped with sarcasm. "And who doesn't like being gagged and tied up?"

"I told you," Tory shrieked, really hysterical now. "It was just a game! Jinx, tell them! Tell them it was just a game!"

I looked at Tory, standing in Petra's tidy, warm living room, looking so incredibly beautiful. She'd always been the prettier one of the two of us.

But I had never resented her for it. I had accepted it, the way you accept that a sister might be taller than you, or a brother better at basketball.

But she had never been able to accept me, and what it was that I had, that she didn't. That she would never, ever have.

The thing was, why should she have accepted it, when for so long, I'd been unable to accept it myself?

But not now. Now, everything was different. *Everything.*

Most of all, me.

"Tell them," Tory begged me, through her tears. "Tell them it was just a game, Jinx."

"No," I said. And this time, when I spoke, I knew they could all understand me.

"No, it wasn't a game, actually."

Which was when Petra, pale but resolute, turned and headed up the stairs—and Tory raced after her, screaming, "No! Petra! I can explain! Wait!"

And Willem, looking confused but determined, went after Tory, apparently to make sure she didn't do anything to Petra.

And then I was alone with Zach.

I was sure Willem's display of devoted chivalry had to sting, so I turned to Zach and said, "I'm sorry."

He looked down at me, clearly surprised. "Sorry? About what? None of this was your fault."

"I don't mean about that," I said. "I mean about Petra. And Willem. I was going to tell you. But I never got a chance. You know." When he continued to look at me blankly, I elaborated: "Zach, I'm sorry. But I don't think they'll be breaking up any time soon. She really loves him. And he really loves her."

Zach's expression, as he gazed down at me, went from one of surprise to one I recognized. It was the same look he'd worn on the baseball field that day—a mix of frustration and amusement.

"Jean," he said. "I don't care about Petra."

"What do you mean, you don't care about her?" I asked, startled. "You love her."

"No," Zach said. "No, I don't. I never did."

"Yes, you did." I sat up a little straighter—then winced, as the motion jostled my sore knee. Still, this was too important to let pass. "You told me you loved her—"

"No," Zach said again. "*You* told *me* that I loved her. Because that fool Robert said so. All I ever said was that there was a time when I found Petra fetching. You were the one who kept going on about it. But the truth is, there's someone else I've been finding a lot more fetching for some time now."

"There is?" I stared up at him in confusion . . . and dismay. "You never told me that."

"No, I didn't," he admitted. "I thought it was easier to just let you go on thinking I loved Petra. Because I could tell you were still freaked over whatever had happened to you, back in Iowa, with that guy. I didn't think you were ready—"

"Ready?" I shook my head. What was he *talking* about? "Ready for what?"

"For me to tell you the truth," Zach said. He was gazing

at me so intently, his green eyes seemed bright as the moon had, outside. "That I had stopped liking Petra the minute I met you." When I continued to look at him blankly, he said, "Out there in that same damned gazebo— the day you arrived. Don't tell me you don't remember."

"Me?" I still didn't think I understood him correctly. "*Me?*"

"Of course *you*," he said, sounding incredulous. "Jean— how could you not have seen it? Tory saw it—why do you think she was so angry? All this time, you've been telling her—me—everyone you knew—that you and I are just friends, when *just friends* was the *last* thing I ever wanted to be with you. And Tory knew it. She could tell what everyone else could, just by looking at me—everyone but you, apparently. That I was head over heels for *you*. . . ." His voice trailed off as he looked down at me. "You still don't believe me, do you?"

How *could* I believe him? How could this be happening—to *me*, of all people?

"That's what I was afraid of," he said, with a sigh. "I guess you've given me no other choice."

"No other choice but . . . *what*?" I squeaked, alarmed.

"This," he said.

And the next thing I knew, his lips were on mine.

I suppose for our first kiss, it was fairly staggering. Well, okay, maybe someone like Tory, who is light-years ahead of me sophistication-wise, could be kissed in such a manner and not completely lose her head.

I, on the other hand, could not. It wasn't as if he

snatched me up and molded my body to his, like Dylan had, the first time he kissed me. Zach's was the gentlest kiss you could ever imagine. He was barely even touching me, except for where his fingers rested on my shoulders.

But while it might have been gentle, it was long. What you might even call lingering.

And I felt it all the way down to my toes.

Oh, I *felt* it.

When he lifted his head again to look at me, I barely noticed. That's because little birds and stars were flying around in front of my eyes, I was so dazzled by the way his mouth had felt on mine.

Thank God I was sitting down. If I'd been standing when he'd kissed me, I'm sure I would have collapsed. I felt as if I were melting. From the inside.

"Now," he asked me, in his deep, quiet voice, "do you believe me?"

But it was hard to formulate a reply, because my lips were tingling so much.

"Okay," Zach said, when I didn't respond right away. "Let me try that again."

And he leaned down to kiss me some more.

This time when he raised his head, birds, stars, and even little rainbows seemed to float around in front of me. It was as if someone had spilled a box of Lucky Charms in zero gravity.

"So?" Zach asked. "Do you believe me now that it's you I love—you that I've *always* loved, ever since that day you spat Long Island iced tea all over me? Do you believe me that I'm tired of trying not to kiss you? Do you believe that I really, really don't want to be *just friends* anymore?"

"Uh-huh," I said, nodding like an idiot.

And then I put my arms around his neck and pulled him toward me. And kissed him some more.

CHAPTER TWENTY-TWO

My knee turned out to be deeply bruised, but not sprained. The doctor said the bruise probably went all the way down to the bone, but that it would fade. Someday.

Sort of like, I hoped, my memory of what had happened that night in the gazebo would fade.

Well, not *all* my memories of that night, of course.

When I went back to Enchantments to thank Lisa for all she'd done for me, and to tell her what had happened—why, for instance, I was using crutches—she'd smiled and said, "So. You did it."

I didn't have to ask what she meant.

"Yes," I'd said. "Yes, I did."

She told me to sleep with lavender beneath my pillow. That it would sweeten my dreams.

It didn't.

But it definitely made my sheets smell better.

What helped, actually, was time. Time and, of course, my friends.

Aunt Evelyn and Uncle Ted were horrified when they heard about what Tory had done to me. But she was still their daughter and, well, they had to stand by her.

Even if she *was* a total whack job.

I could sympathize. And it wasn't as if she'd been trying to kill me.

I'm pretty sure.

Tory had just meant to drink a few drops of my blood, absorb whatever it was she was so convinced I'd inherited that she hadn't, force me to drink some noxious potion she'd concocted from some toadstools off a gravestone, and then let me go.

At least, that's what she told her parents would have happened, if Zach hadn't barged in.

I guess I believe her. I mean, it's the same story Lindsey and Gretchen told THEIR parents.

But they, of course, were hardly likely to admit they'd been accomplices to attempted murder.

Really, the only question I had about the whole thing was . . . well, the one I put to Zach the next day. I was home from the doctor's office with an ice pack on my knee, sitting in the den in front of the TV while Mr. and Mrs. Gardiner were at Tory's therapists . . . with Tory, of course.

That question was: How had he known? About what

was going on in the gazebo.

"I was up," he said. "I couldn't sleep." He leveled a wry smile in my direction. "I think you know why."

"That," I said, for what seemed like the millionth time, "was Tory's doll, not—"

"—yours. I know. Gretchen said as much last night, remember? Anyway, I was up, and . . . I don't remember exactly—oh, I heard a cat crying. It must have been Mouche—"

"It was," I said. Mouche was safely back with Alice, who'd been kept from the knowledge that her beloved pet had been used in such a dangerous manner.

"Right. Well, that's when I looked down and noticed the lights in the gazebo. And I just thought it was . . . weird. You know, that there should be candles burning in the gazebo. Also that Mouche should be out so late. So I went downstairs and hopped the wall between our two gardens to take a look. As I walked over, I heard that crazy stuff Tory was saying to you. Then I walked in and saw . . . well, you know what I saw."

I nodded. Yes. I knew what he'd seen.

And also what he'd heard.

Mouche, yes. But also, me. He'd heard *me*.

He didn't know it. He would probably never know it. But that was all right.

For now.

"But if you knew that doll wasn't mine all along," I asked him, "why didn't you say anything? At the dance, I mean?"

"You left so fast, how could I? I tried to come by later, too, but Petra said you'd gone to bed. Anyway, I knew you hadn't made the doll," he said, "because I know you. You always tell the truth—well, except for that fib about buying that book for your sister Courtney's birthday." I blushed—prettily, I hoped. But still. "Which you eventually fessed up to. You admitted you made the Dylan doll, and it was easy to tell the two dolls hadn't been made by the same person."

I should hope so. I mean, I totally got an A in sewing in the seventh grade. Whereas Tory's Zach doll . . . well, you could tell it had been made by someone who'd never so much as woven a pot holder.

"So I knew you hadn't tried to put a love spell on me using a stupid doll," Zach went on. "But . . . well, earlier in the day, I did find something kind of weird in my back-pack—"

And he pulled, from the pocket of his jeans, the little bag Lisa had made for me.

"That's for protection," I said. "I was worried Tory might try to do something to you. You're supposed to keep it with you, and then nothing bad will happen to you."

He looked down at the bag, and nodded.

"I suspected something like that," he said, returning it to his pocket. "But I wasn't sure."

Then I realized what he meant.

"Wait . . . you didn't think it was a love potion, or something, did you?" I asked, turning crimson.

"Well," he said. "I *was* having trouble getting you out of my head. So it did cross my mind that maybe—"

"Zach!" I cried, sitting up—and jostling my knee. "I would never—I told you, I learned my lesson with Dylan! I will never, ever do another love spell for as long as I live."

"I know," he said, with a laugh. "I loved you way before you ever had a chance to put a spell on me. I loved you at *I've never been to Long Island*."

I couldn't keep a big goofy grin from my face.

"I loved you at *I like seals*," I admitted.

He grinned back. "And anyway," he went on, "you know I don't believe all that witchcraft mumbo-jumbo. I told you that."

"I know you don't," I said. "But you have to admit . . ." How could I put this? "The whole thing with Dylan—"

"You said it yourself. He was a guy primed to fall in love, and you showed up at just the right time."

"Yes," I said. "But then how do you explain me pushing you out of the way of that bike messenger?"

"Same thing. Right place, wrong time," Zach said.

"And last night? Zach, how can you even begin to explain last night?"

"Which part? The part where your psycho cousin tried to drain your blood so she could inherit some of your dead grandma's magic? Or the part where I rescued you?"

"The second part," I said. "How did you know to look

out the window *right then?*"

"I told you," he said. "I heard Alice's cat."

The cat? Or me?

Or . . . Branwen?

"Anyway," Zach said, with a shrug, "we're even now, you know. I no longer owe you eternal servitude. You saved me from being run over by a bike, and now I saved you from your psychotic cousin. And speaking of psychotic, what happened to that Dylan guy, anyway?"

"The Gardiners put him on a plane back to Iowa this morning," I said, with a sigh.

I realized I would never get Zach to admit there might be such a thing as magic. Oh, well. He'd find out for himself, eventually. If he hung around with me long enough, anyway. Of that, I had no doubt.

"They found him staying at the Waldorf," I said. "Dylan, I mean. Tory used one of their credit cards to get him a room—not to mention the plane ticket. He spent five hundred dollars on room service and pay-per-view alone."

"Wow," Zach said. "You sure know how to pick 'em."

I threw one of the pillows from the couch at him. He caught it with a laugh and said, "You must be feeling better." Then he settled onto the couch beside me—careful of my sore knee—and leaned over until his face was just an inch or two from mine.

"Hey, Jean," he said, much more softly.

I looked up at his lips. "Yes?"

"I have a feeling"—now Zach was looking down at *my*

lips—"no one's going to be calling you Jinx anymore. I think from now on, your luck's going to be taking a turn for the better."

Then he kissed me.

Oddly enough, it turned out Zach was right. About my luck taking a turn for the better after that. For instance, the Chapman School scholarship that Zach told me about?

Well, I auditioned for it.

And I got it.

Then, of course, there was the awkward part . . . asking Aunt Evelyn and Uncle Ted if I could stay with them for the next school year.

But from the way they reacted, it was clear it had never occurred to them that I might even have *wanted* to go back to Hancock. I was a member of the family now—*their* family—and I was welcome to stay as long as I wanted.

This might have been on account of the fact that it was Tory, in the end, who left . . . for juvenile boot camp, where she got to spend the rest of her sophomore year, as well as her summer vacation. And then, when she got back—her dyed black hair gone, and a new fuzz of her natural blond hair covering her head like the fluff on a baby chick—her parents had a surprise: they'd enrolled her in a "specialty" boarding school, instead of Chapman, for her junior year.

And even though Tory accused them of shipping her off to military school, that wasn't true. Not at all. The school they sent her to was a beautiful camp in—of all places—rural Iowa, where students did things like run a farm, go on nature hikes, and basically challenge themselves in ways they'd never been challenged before. In other words . . .

They learned to embrace their fears.

On a daily basis.

It wasn't easy for Aunt Evelyn and Uncle Ted to send Tory there. But, as Aunt Evelyn put it, she had Teddy and Alice to worry about, and she didn't feel like Tory was exactly the best role model in the world for them.

And the nice thing about the place where they sent Tory? She could stay with *my* family on the weekends.

That's right. Tory got to visit Hancock every Saturday and Sunday, and see what being a kid in a preacher's house was all about.

According to Chanelle, to whom Tory occasionally wrote, Tory found life in my house even harder than boot camp.

She did have one person to comfort her in her misery, however.

With Dylan coming home every weekend from Iowa State, and Tory there in Hancock every weekend, well . . . I guess it was only natural that love would bloom.

At least if Courtney's last e-mail—complaining that Dylan and Tory are constantly being busted by Mom for making out in the TV room—is to be believed.

And despite what Zach might think, I had nothing to do with it. After all, I promised Zach that I've sworn off love spells.

I really meant it, too. Because the best, most long-lasting love has a magic all its own, and doesn't need any help from witchcraft.

Zach was right about one other thing, too:

No one calls me Jinx anymore. Now it's just Jean. Plain old Jean.

And I actually like it that way.